D0988181

Praise for *The Wrong Heaven*

'Incredibly fun to read but also full of these **frank and wise** observations that stuck in my head long after'
Aimee Bender, *New York Times* bestselling author of *The Particular Sadness of Lemon Cake*

'In her **amazing, wildly inventive** collection, Amy Bonnaffons writes about transformation, each story further complicating the world as we know it. With a style that **blends humor and sincerity in such strange, perfect ratios**, Bonnaffons reveals the mysteries inside of us, just waiting to make themselves known. *The Wrong Heaven*, so wondrous, will alter you in all the necessary ways'
Kevin Wilson, author of *The Family Fang*

'**Amy Bonnaffons is the real deal**. She's a woman of impossible juxtapositions. Funny and wise, thrilling and disciplined, strange and masterful. **Do yourself a favor and read this**: you'll be surprised where you find yourself, but you'll never feel lost'
Darin Strauss, author of *Chang & Eng*

'God, these stories. I wanted to stop people on the street. I know contemporary writers who can lacerate, and I know others who are funny, and I even know some who can pull off pathos. But I don't know any who can do all three at once – with mastery, mischief, and meaning – like Amy Bonnaffons. **She gives you a key to that secret room where, for a dear second, everything stops moving so quickly and you get a glimpse of the truth**'

Boris Fishman, author of *Don't Let Me Baby Do Rodeo*

'These stories are **eerie, enthralling, and hilarious**. Women grow hooves, carve dolls who talk, have sex (or almost) with angels. **Bonnaffons is a masterful chronicler of female desire and its discontents**'

Leni Zumas, author of *Red Clocks*

'Like the best storytelling, *The Wrong Heaven* feels like a gift – **warm, intimate, and very, very funny**. The characters are messy and vibrant and gloriously flawed, and their transformations are absolutely enthralling. This **energizing** collection will stay with me – happily so – for a long time. Read it'

Kayla Rae Whitaker, author of *The Animators*

'At once **goofy, poignant, and edged with the fantastic**, the stories in Bonnaffons's debut collection initially surprise, then turn into one long, delicious rush. **Not just fun but full of smart ideas**'

Library Journal starred review

THE WRONG HEAVEN

Amy Bonnaffons is a founding editor of *7x7.la*, a literary journal devoted to collaborations between writers and visual artists. Born in New York City, she now lives in Athens, GA, where she is working on a Ph.D. at the University of Georgia. She holds a B.A. from Yale University and a M.F.A. from New York University.

THE

WRONG HEAVEN

AMY BONNAFFONS

WEIDENFELD & NICOLSON

First published in Great Britain in 2018
by Weidenfeld & Nicolson
an imprint of The Orion Publishing Group Ltd
Carmelite House, 50 Victoria Embankment
London EC4Y 0DZ

An Hachette UK Company

1 3 5 7 9 10 8 6 4 2

A CIP catalogue record for this book is
available from the British Library.

ISBN (Mass Market Paperback) 978 1 4746 1023 0
ISBN (eBook) 978 1 4746 1024 7

www.orionbooks.co.uk

For my parents

CONTENTS

THE WRONG HEAVEN

THE WRONG HEAVEN

Evidence in Favor of Jesus Being on My Side:

1. Word of God, as appears in Bible (obv.)
2. Tomatoes
3. Pipe organs
4. Meditative feeling brought on by needlepoint
5. Rodgers & Hammerstein
6. Jacqueline Kennedy Onassis (existence)
7. flowers / constant renewal of life cycle
8. Billie Holiday (singer)
9. Billie Holiday (dog)
10. Theory that everything exists for purpose, pain and trouble sent as trials, all to bring us closer to God, etc.
11. Way students say "Oh!" when pet caterpillars turn into butterflies

Evidence Against:

1. Genocide / wanton destruction
2. Insomnia
3. Evolution
4. Animal cruelty
5. Jacqueline Kennedy Onassis (world's treatment of)
6. Dimpled thighs
7. General lack of love in life
8. Early death of Billie Holiday (singer)
9. Early death of Billie Holiday (dog)
10. Dream in which I slap Jesus's face
11. Dream in which Jesus slaps my face
12. Dreams in which Jesus and I sit mutely on folding chairs in a blank room, as in group therapy, but with no therapist, wanting to slap each other's face but unable to rouse ourselves to action
13. Looks on students' faces when caterpillars die unexpectedly
14. Looks on students' faces when caterpillars die expectedly (different and somehow worse)

Evidence Against seemed to grow longer every day. Plus, a growing number of items appeared on both lists.

So on my lunch break, I went and bought some new lawn ornaments. Neither Home Depot nor Safeway had the kind I wanted; the Safeway guy referred me to a place called Tony's Catholic Bonanza, on the East Side.

I arrived back at school out of breath, four minutes late, carrying an Electric Jesus and a Flashing Virgin.

My class was waiting for me at their little desks with folded hands, like anxious orphans. They're the "remedial" class (as opposed to "regular" or "gifted"), and they know it; they're always afraid of being one step behind, of discovering that something that seems like a joke will turn out not to be.

"Who's ready for marine-life dioramas?" I sang. I placed the lawn ornaments on my desk and hung my purse on the back of my chair. Then I plugged in Jesus and Mary, because I thought this would cheer them. But two of the children immediately started to cry.

I unplugged the statues, and made a mental note to add this to Evidence Against.

I stayed late to grade spelling tests, but I couldn't focus. Jesus and Mary kept staring at me.

It's not that they were lifelike—they were made of shoddy translucent plastic, their features colored in with already-flaking paint. But there was something about them. Mary had a calm, serene expression on her paper-white face, her large imploring eyes floating above her swimming-pool-blue robes, her palms folded demurely across her middle. Jesus, on the other hand, had a sort of intense, burning stare. He held His white-robed arms out to the side in a way that could have been an embrace or a pantomime of crucifixion—I wasn't sure. I'd never thought about how similar the two looked.

I leaned over and plugged them in. The electric glow shot through their translucent skin, and they lit up like fireflies against the dusky room.

"You are loved," said Mary.

"Probably," said Jesus.

"We know you have questions," said Mary. "And we have answers."

"But we're not just going to give them away for free," said Jesus. He held out His palms. "Look at the marks where the nails went in."

I grimaced.

"Come on," said Mary. She shot Jesus a reproachful glance. "We've talked about this." Then she smiled sweetly. "So," she said. "How can we help you today, Cheryl?"

"Well," I said. "I guess I'd just like to feel like you're on my side."

Mary nodded sympathetically. "I think you're doing a bang-up job," she said, "under the circumstances." She had a slight British accent, like Julie Andrews.

"Look," said Jesus. "Don't take it the wrong way, what I'm about to say. It's just my personality. But have you considered the lilies of the field? The birds, and wild beasts? Do *they* wonder who's on 'their side'?" He made air quotes.

"I don't know," I said.

"They don't," he said.

I waited for Him to say something more, but He didn't. He just stood there with His arms folded, apparently waiting for me to say something. Mary rolled her eyes.

I leaned over and unplugged them. Their lights went out, and their faces hardened into frozen masks of cheap colored plastic.

I picked them up, took them out to the car, and drove back to Tony's Catholic Bonanza.

"They don't work?" said the young man behind the counter. He had eyes as green as marbles, and black hair neatly parted down the middle.

"They work," I said. "That's not the problem. The problem is, they're judgmental."

He nodded. "Ah, I see," he said. He folded his arms. "A lot of people complain about that."

"So can you take them back?"

"No, ma'am." He shook his head. He pointed to a large handwritten sign that said NO REFUNDS ON STATUES.

I sighed. "Where do these come from, anyway?"

"Papa's Plastics. It's the only factory located partially inside the Vatican City."

"What do you mean, partially?"

"Half of it is and half of it isn't. Vatican City is very small. They make statues and rosary beads and shovels. For burying the dead."

"*Plastic* shovels?"

He shrugged. "The soil is very loose in that part of Italy. Anyway, it's all been blessed by the Pope."

"What do you mean, blessed? Does he sprinkle holy water on it or something?"

"No, but his car drives by the factory sometimes and he gives a little wave." He demonstrated by limply raising his hand, then letting it drop.

I sighed. "Thanks for your help." I picked up the two statues, one under each arm, and headed back out to the car.

When I got home, I placed Mary and Jesus in front of the rosebush, which provided a nice color contrast with her blue robes and His white ones. I did not plug them in.

Instead, I went into the kitchen and opened the freezer. There was Billie Holiday. She was in a plastic bag, but I could clearly see the shape of her through it. One of her little paws stuck out of the bottom. She had died a month ago, but I still couldn't bring myself to move her. I stood in front of the freezer and looked at her for a while. Then, I reached to the left of her stiff body, took out the gin, and closed the door. I filled a glass nearly to the top, and threw in a little tonic water. I took one delicious sip and then went over to the living room, lay down on the rug, and tried to balance the glass on my chest. I had read about someone doing this, in a novel or something. It was harder than it looked. When I breathed, the glass tipped forward and spilled down my front, soaking my torso and crotch.

Lately, everything was harder than it looked. Things had turned out so disappointingly for me. Beauty had not turned into happiness. It hadn't even turned into beauty (see, in Evidence Against, item 6: Dimpled thighs).

I shouldn't have been so stuck up in the bloom of my youth. I turned away six objectively impressive men. They were all just so boring. But it's also boring, I now realize, to be alone.

Let me tell you about Billie Holiday. I'm not even a dog person. But when I saw her face on the flyer, I knew she was mine.

The flyer was on the bulletin board at ShopRite. It said FREE DOG, and underneath there was a picture. She was an unclassifiable mutt, with deep cocker-spaniel eyes and matted terrier fur and a wrinkled bulldog brow; she looked both anxious and mournful. My heart lay down, rolled over.

I didn't rip off one of the detachable slips at the bottom, I just took the whole poster. I even took the thumbtack. I'm not sure why. I called the number and drove over immediately.

The owner's directions took me to a trailer on the edge of the woods outside of town. A woman answered the front door. (Is "front door" the right term, or are trailer doors defined like car doors, driver and passenger?) She was extremely pregnant, but also extremely fat.

You couldn't even have told except that the roundness of her belly had a convex tautness, a definition that the rest of her lacked. The rest of her was slack, weary, blurred. Two small children played on the floor in diapers.

"There she is," said the woman. She gestured toward a card table that apparently served as the family's combination dining room table and changing pad. A bowl of congealed SpaghettiOs stood next to a steaming diaper. Beneath the table, Billie Holiday cowered, shaking like a leaf.

I crouched down. "Come here, darling," I said. The dog took a tentative step forward, then retreated. She began to whimper.

"She's a nice dog," said the woman. I looked up at her. Her hands rested on her high belly. Her eyes were even sadder than the bowl of SpaghettiOs, which is saying a lot. "Not much trouble. But my boyfriend said *someone* had to go." She looked down at her belly and shrugged.

I coaxed Billie Holiday out of the corner and picked her up. She stared into my eyes with a humanlike intensity. It was clear what her eyes were saying. They were saying: *I still have hope.* They were big, quivering, Liza Minnelli eyes.

But I didn't name her Liza. I didn't name her anything until a week later, when I put on "Lady Sings the Blues," and I watched her stop what she was doing—which was batting around a toy rubber martini glass I'd bought her—and *listen*. She actually listened. She cocked her head to the side and her ears perked up. Then—and here's the amazing part—*she closed her eyes.*

I watched her listen to the rest of the song, with her eyes closed. When it was over, she lay down and fell asleep. In her dog-dreams, she moaned a low dog-moan, full of tenderness and pain.

I played the song several times that week, and always the same thing happened. And so I had no choice, name-wise. Billie she was, and Billie she would always be. Until last month, when she died of dog leukemia. That's when I started making the list. Because what kind of God would give leukemia to a *dog*? I often tell my students to marvel at the small and myriad wonders of the world. A caterpillar's many feet, the tiny veins of a leaf. I have them look at the veins in their hand, then back at the leaf. Hand. Leaf. Hand. Leaf. After a while, are they that different? Does it matter? I don't say this, because it would be anti–separation of church and state, but I believe— or want to believe—that the world is full of these mira-cles, little filigrees personally added by the Creator. But that would mean that the self-same Creator also came up with dog leukemia. And what kind of a filigree is that?

I fell asleep that night on the living room floor, in front of *World's Most Interesting Autopsies.* In the morning, when I pulled myself up and went outside, my clothes were stiff with the gin and tonic; it had soaked through them and dried overnight.

I stared at the statues for a moment, then plugged in only Mary. I couldn't deal with the other one right now.

"Good morning," she said. "Sorry about yesterday. He sometimes gets carried away."

"It's OK," I said. "I was a bit rattled, though."

"You poor thing," she said.

"Can you answer some questions for me?"

"Maybe later," she said. "Right now, I'd rather sing." She took a breath and began: *"There's a bright golden haze on the meadow ..."*

It was "Oh, What a Beautiful Mornin'" from *Okla-homa!*, which is one of my favorite songs, which she probably knew. But her voice was wispy and wavering, and she was a little flat on the high notes. Plus, it sounded odd and wrong with her British accent. Still, I thought it would be rude to interrupt her. So I stood and listened until she finished.

"Thank you," I said. "That was lovely."

She smiled and gave a slight nod and curtsy. I unplugged her and went inside to get ready for school.

In case you're wondering, I wasn't *that* surprised that they could talk. My view of the universe is Christian but not narrow. On TV once, I saw an elephant and a dog who were best friends; the elephant rubbed the dog's belly with its foot. A woman in my church had a horseback-riding accident and saw the white light at the end of the tunnel, and after they brought her back she was able to accurately predict the results of every midterm Senate election. My brother James had a spiritual conversion in his twenties and is now a Yoruba priest. Anything can happen.

This is why my students like me, why I've received the highest ratings of any second-grade teacher at Two Trees Elementary for eighteen years straight: I believe the world is malleable, that our understanding of it is provisional, improvised, subject to a change of rules at any time; that sometimes the magician pulls out the tablecloth and the dishes all stay in place, and sometimes the magician pulls out the tablecloth and everything is gone, including the table. I don't tell the children how things are. I don't condescend.

But lately, it's all too much. I'm starting to believe that maybe, like other adults, I should start pretending to know more than I do. I don't know a single other adult who recently woke up in gin-stiffened clothes clutching a rubber martini-shaped dog toy. I would not wish this on anyone.

That day, one of my students turned eight. Her mother brought in cupcakes for everyone. There were so many allergies in the room that parents weren't allowed to bring in anything with peanuts, wheat, sugar, milk, pineapple, shellfish, strawberries, soy, or Red Dye No. 9. Among other things. What remained was basically spelt flour and water. The cupcakes were made with spelt flour and water and they tasted like spelt flour and water. The children and I played a game while eating them where we imagined a world without allergies. We discussed what we would eat for people's birthdays in this allergy-free world.

"Chicken nuggets," said one.

"Soy sauce," said another.

"Red eggs and ham," said the child allergic to red dye.

"What if there was this magic dinosaur," said Maddox, my favorite, "that ate everything in the world and vomited it back up, but its vomit was actually really delicious food with no allergies?"

Caroline N. raised her hand. "What would the dinosaur keep in its stomach?"

"Excuse me?" I said.

"If it vomits everything up, it doesn't get to keep anything in its own stomach."

"I guess it dies," said Maddox. He looked stricken. He clearly had not considered this question.

"Like my caterpillar," said Josephine. "My caterpillar died."

"My baby brother died," said David G., "before he was born."

I looked out at the sea of faces grown round with fear, spelt crumbs strewing them like dark freckles.

"Nobody dies for real, ever," I pronounced. "There's just a different place where dead people go. Like how we can't see Ms. McClosky's class right now, but we know they're next door."

My students looked relieved, even hopeful; Ms. Mc-Closky's class was "gifted."

When I got home, it was dark already. I poured myself a G&T, drank it standing up, and then poured another. I went outside and plugged the statues into the outlet at the base of the porch. They lit up against the darkness.

"I saw what you just did," said Jesus. "I saw how strong you made that drink."

"You are loved," said Mary. But she sounded a little strained.

"I was just a normal human like you, and I got through life's trials without stimulants or depressants," said Jesus. "Do you need to see my hands again?"

"You don't need to keep reminding people," said Mary.

"It was very traumatic," said Jesus.

"Look," I said. "I'm a mess. I admit it. And the worst part is, I'm supposed to be *guiding* people."

"How can we help?" asked Mary, smiling and spreading her hands.

"Well," I said, "for starters, I would feel better if I just knew that there was a Heaven. That Billie Holiday was in a better place. And the caterpillars, and David G.'s baby brother."

"It's not so much like that," said Jesus. "It's not really another place."

Mary cleared her throat. "Let me explain it to you,"

she said. "Think of caterpillars. Hedgehogs. Carrots. Dogs. Babies. There's a Heaven for each one, and they all exist in the same airspace, like all the radio signals from all the world flying through the air, constantly. But you need the right equipment. Is your Heavenly Radio tuned to the right station? You might be picking up Carrot Heaven, or Hedgehog Heaven."

"The radio is a metaphor," said Jesus. "The metaphors are given out at birth, like names. Some people get the wrong ones. You can get another, at Customer Service, but there's no escalator. This is the only body you've ever had. Use it, and walk up the stairs. You get to Heaven by willpower and thigh muscle."

"Call this toll-free number from a touch-tone phone," said Mary, "if you believe you've selected the wrong Heaven for your species, gender, socioeconomic status, and weight class. You are loved. You are loved. You are loved."

"Possibly," said Jesus.

I turned and walked inside, without unplugging them. I lay on the couch and felt their faint glow through the curtain. I couldn't believe that Jesus had mentioned my thighs.

Outside, Mary softly murmured the toll-free number, over and over and over. I got up and called it.

It was busy.

I went into the kitchen and opened up the freezer. I

took out the gin bottle, but it was empty. I stood there with the bottle in my hand, tapping its cold heft against my thigh, trying to decide whether it was worth a trip to the liquor store. Then my eyes fixed on Billie Holiday.

I thought about how we used to spend time here together, doing the dishes. I'd taught her to stand on the counter with a clean towel wrapped around her; I'd rub the dishes against her towel-clad body to dry them. She loved to help out. She loved the attention, and the togetherness.

No one knew about that but she and I. No one but me could remember. The responsibility was mine, and no one would help me with it: not even Our Lord and the Holy Mother. They might know about the various levels and frequencies of Heaven, but I was the only one who could lay my friend to rest in the earth.

I knew what I had to do.

When I got to the store, its door was shut and the lights were off. But when I peered through the glass door, I could see one light on in the back—probably in some sort of storage closet—and the silhouette of someone moving around.

I rapped strongly on the door. The silhouette stopped and stood still. I knocked again, and in a few seconds the green-eyed man was at the door.

He turned the lock and opened it. "We're closed," he said.

"I know," I said. "But I really need your help."

"With what?"

"I want one of your shovels."

He sighed. "Why do people always wait till the middle of the night to decide they need one of those?" He stepped aside. "Come in."

I came in. He pulled a string, and a lightbulb on the ceiling clicked on. "Wait here," he said. "I'll go get one from the back. Which color do you want? We have white, blue, and black."

"Black," I said. He disappeared into the back for a moment, then returned carrying a black plastic shovel, about as long as my forearm. The image of a single wing was embedded on the flat part.

I looked up at him. His eyes flamed like emeralds. A small pool of light encircled us against the hot, breathless dark.

"What's your name?" I asked.

"Why should I tell you?"

"Because I want to know."

He shrugged. "Felix," he said. "Felix Ramirez Johnson."

"Felix," I said, "can I ask you something?"

"Go ahead."

"Will you be my witness?"

"Your what?"

"I'm going to hold a funeral, right now. For my dog, in my backyard. And I need a witness."

Felix looked like he had seen everything. He shrugged. "I'll get my coat," he said.

In the car, I said, "So. Felix. Where are you from? Mexico?"

"Actually," he said, "I'm Nicaraguan. But I was born here."

"Oh. Nicaragua. Is that where they have the Galápagos Islands? With the turtles?"

"No, that's Ecuador."

"Oh." I pulled into the driveway. Mary and Jesus were still lit up in front of the rosebushes.

"Well," said Felix, "they *look* nice."

"Thanks," I said. "But they're really just being such bullies."

He nodded. "I know what you mean."

As we approached the statues, Mary said, "You've brought a friend!"

"What's up, Felix," said Jesus. He gave a little nod.

"Sorry, guys," said Felix. "I'm gonna unplug you." He reached out and pulled their cords, and that was that.

Felix and I took turns with the black shovel. It was a surprisingly excellent instrument. It felt good to dig, and to watch him dig; different combinations of muscles surfaced in his arms as he moved the shovel up and down. We had a hole in no time.

I had chosen a lovely spot beneath the oak tree in my backyard, and when the hole was large enough, I placed

Billie inside. I'd dressed her in her favorite tartan rain jacket and boots, and wrapped her in her favorite blanket. I threw in the rubber martini glass and my copy of "Lady Sings the Blues." Then I stood back up and folded my hands. There was a feeling of momentousness in the air. Something important was happening. And I had no idea what to say.

"I should say a prayer," I said, finally. "A eulogy, I guess."

"Sure," said Felix.

"Before these witnesses," I began. "Before these witnesses, God and Felix Ramirez Johnson…"

Felix stood with his head bowed respectfully. How was I supposed to continue?

"Before these witnesses," I said again. "Before these—"

And then I burst into tears.

Felix stood there, doing nothing, while my sobs exploded like wet fireworks down my face and clothes. Or rather, he wasn't doing nothing. He just wasn't moving. But I could tell something was taking place within him; he was paying attention to my sobs, listening to them, as if he were a scientist in the wild, and they were the cries of some elusive animal, and they carried a great and indiscernible meaning.

Felix let me cry until I stopped. It was a long time.

"The day my parents were murdered," he said, finally, "I didn't feel anything at all. And I haven't felt anything since."

We stood there, staring down at the grave. We stood there until it felt like the grave was staring back at us. Then, our eyes glazed over and lost focus and we weren't looking at anything anymore. We turned and went inside.

"There's one more thing I need help with, before you go," I told Felix, filling up two glasses of water.

"What?"

"Well, I feel like I need to get rid of Jesus and Mary."

"Hm."

"No hard feelings," I said. "They just make things more confusing."

"Fair enough."

"And since you can't take them back," I continued, "I need to destroy them."

He nodded, and folded his arms. "Tell me what you're thinking."

I told him what I was thinking.

"I see," he said, nodding slowly. "I'm not sure about the plastic."

"But it's special plastic," I said. "The Pope waved at it."

"True," he said, and shrugged.

We went and got the statues from the front of the house and brought them around to the backyard. I got the can of kerosene from the garage and the fire extinguisher from the kitchen, and Felix pulled a book of matches out of his coat pocket. I doused the statues in the liquid; he lit a match and tossed it.

Jesus and Mary blossomed instantly into flame. I let them burn for a few seconds—just long enough to see their features begin to melt—and then I sprayed them down.

Mary stood there dripping, her body charred and singed like an overgrilled hot dog. But Jesus continued to burn.

I looked over at Felix; we locked eyes for a moment, and then he turned and ran into the house and emerged with a pitcher of water. He dumped the water onto Jesus. The water cascaded over and around the flames, but He continued to burn.

Felix and I worked as a team. He went back and forth from the kitchen, getting more water; I continued to soak the statue. But no matter how many times we drenched Him, He would not stop burning. Finally, we stopped trying.

"Well," said Felix. "I've never seen *this* before." He took a step back. "It's not stopping, but it's not catching anything else, either."

It was true. The fire did not spread. Even Mary, next to Him, appeared flameproof. She just stood there, palms folded demurely, her face thoroughly charred.

Felix slowly approached the flaming Jesus. He contemplated it for a moment. Then he stuck his hand right into the flame, and held it there.

I screamed. He removed his hand. It was perfect and smooth and untouched.

"Well," I said. "What should we do?"

He shrugged his signature shrug. "I guess we should make the best of it."

Suddenly, I knew exactly what that meant. "I'll be right back," I said.

Felix and I spent the night in front of the flaming Jesus, marshmallows speared on long sticks snapped from the oak tree, roasting them in Our Lord's flames. The backyard was dark, and He was our only light.

"I can't believe you'd never had s'mores before," I said.

"They're really good," he admitted. He put another marshmallow on his stick and extended it into the flames. Instantly, the whole thing caught fire; he removed it and blew it down, revealing a dry blackened lump. He looked up and made a sheepish face.

"Don't worry about that," I said. "The most important thing, no matter what happens on the outside, is to keep the inside tender. You can always peel away the surface. There's always another layer underneath."

I watched as he removed the charred exterior, flake by blackened flake. "Here goes," he said. Then, he slowly extended the naked quivering mass toward the fire, and held it at exactly the right distance from the burning Jesus. We both watched as the alchemy took hold: the marshmallow's skin slowly turning into gold, kissed again and again by the edge of the flame.

THE OTHER ONE

As far as I could tell, I was the only customer at Joyful-SongTime. Again. This was the third day in a row I had spent my lunch break here, and I had yet to encounter another person, aside from the teenage attendant who'd swiped my credit card and then solemnly handed me a sparkly tambourine.

I didn't even like karaoke. I had come here for a very specific reason: to sing one song and one song only, over and over again, until I was hoarse. The goal was a kind of immersion therapy. The goal was to sing Alanis Morissette's "Hand in My Pocket" until it lost its hold on me.

Why "Hand in My Pocket"? I had no idea. Believe me, I had tried to figure it out, why this song of all the songs in the world should have woken me in the middle of the night, and then *stayed*. I'd had songs in my head before, of course. But this song inhabited me. It blared so loudly through my consciousness that I couldn't focus on the briefs I had to write, couldn't help but walk in time with its beat, pace my thinking to its slow loopy cadence.

I couldn't afford the distraction. I was planning a wedding, and I had dozens of billable hours ahead of me. I worked at the kind of Midtown law firm where people *actually* said things like "I need this done yesterday!" I got the sense that if an associate lost focus noticeably enough, the partners would take her into a quiet back conference room, where she would be discreetly beheaded. Our clients were the people who owned America, America's version of kings. They'd tolerate no slack, no whimsy.

'Cause I've got one hand in my pocket, and the other one is giving a high five.

I hadn't intended to end up at a place like McNally, Bose & Gold. I went to law school with noble civic intentions; I wanted to be Erin Brockovich. But then I joined the firm to pay off my loans, and discovered my own deep veins of masochism and venality. It became addictive to tap those veins, to discover new veins when the original ones had become depleted through overuse. I succumbed to a pleasurable moral swoon. I began to indulge in other activities I'd previously disdained: spin classes, boozy brunches, adultery. When the married partner I'd been fucking left his wife to be with me, it seemed like my new, self-centered worldview had triumphed.

Now, a year and a half later, Dennis and I were engaged. I had always claimed, for feminist reasons, that if I ever got married I would forgo a white wedding dress, but that was before I saw myself refracted in the mirrored bridal dressing room at Bloomingdale's, in a gown with a plunging front and lacy back, looking like a beautiful stranger, like the kind of woman I previously never would have even bothered to envy because she was so completely of another realm, apart in her feathery grace from the clunk and sweat of daily reality. I had done the impossible, what everyone wants to do: I had become a different person.

Then, about a week after my dress fitting, I awoke with an ache in my abdomen and a shocking river of blood between my legs. My periods had always been irregular, but usually they came on more gently; this flood was sudden and absolute. Biblical. I rinsed and replaced the sheets (luckily, Dennis had already left for work), plugged myself with a tampon, and dragged my sluggish, sodden self to the office—but after a few hours I gave up and left to work from home. I was extracting a saturated tampon twice an hour. Was this body really the same graceful, confectionary thing I'd seen in the Bloomingdale's mirror last week? I couldn't believe what it seemed to be saying about itself, that it could spew forth such carnage.

When I got home, I took my laptop to bed with a bar of chocolate and a hot water bottle. At first this was a relief, but I soon found myself wrenched by a sudden, crippling sadness. I curled up in the fetal position for an hour, uncurling myself only to pull open my laptop and Google *am i having a miscarriage???*

The thought had occurred to me suddenly, with an inner shock of something-like-certainty, but the Internet could not tell me for sure. It wasn't likely that I could have gotten pregnant (I was on birth control) but it was possible (I'd missed a day here and there). I'd certainly never bled like this before. I debated calling my gynecologist, I debated calling Dennis, but in the end I did neither.

I didn't even tell Dennis my suspicion when he got home and asked, with tender boyfriendly solicitude, how I was feeling. By then the bleeding had slowed to a trickle. I simply moaned and turned over onto my stomach and accepted his offer of a back rub. My head was turned to the side and I could see our reflection in the window: a woman prone on her bed, her caramel-colored hair spilling out over the pillow, while a tall handsome man tenderly strokes her back. It was a nice picture. The whole idea suddenly seemed impossible and ridiculous, the idea that I might have had a miscarriage. It didn't fit. I felt faintly embarrassed about the whole thing. I murmured *Thank you* to Dennis, and something like *You're the best*, and something involving *love*.

The next morning, when I woke up, my belly had stopped aching, and Dennis's heavy arm lay across my body like a caveman's club, and I felt protected and out of danger and blissfully sane. At work I was myself again. That night we drank a bottle of wine and I gave him a blow job that made me feel like the blow job champion of the world, like a real winner. Things were back to normal.

Then, in the middle of the night, it started: the song. It woke me at 3 a.m., pounding through my head like an insistent revelation, preventing me from sleeping until morning.

The teenage attendant led me down the hall and showed me into the dim cave of room 6: small and dark, with padded vinyl couches and swirling disco lights. He went through the same routine I'd seen several times already, the silent flight-attendant-style pointing, showing me the binders full of laminated lists of song titles, the remote I would use to enter their identifying numbers, the button I would press if I wanted to order some beer or shrimp-flavored chips.

"Have a joyful song time," he whispered. Then he exited the room, shuffling backwards, pulling the door shut behind him.

I sat down, entered the familiar six digits, and heard the opening strains of "Hand in My Pocket": not the actual Alanis song but the bubbly karaoke version, accompanied by video images of a blond couple strolling down a Parisian boulevard, both wearing flippy '90s-era hats and laughing heartily, heads thrown back, as if the streets of Paris were inherently hilarious. I now knew this couple intimately; they had transcended their initial ridiculousness and come to seem inevitable, as if they had emerged directly from my unconscious, as if I had dreamed them myself.

My first lunch break at JoyfulSongTime, I'd tried to push the song out of my head by replacing it. I sang sexy songs with frank lyrics ("Drunk in Love," "I Touch Myself," "Why Don't We Do It in the Road?"). I sang ballads of naked self-pity ("All by Myself," "I Can't Make You Love Me," "November Rain"). I sang songs I secretly loved ("Total Eclipse of the Heart") and secretly hated ("Call Your Girlfriend"). For about five minutes after I left, my head was blessedly silent. But within a few blocks, she was there again, Alanis: yelping about high fives and cigarettes, musically distilling the paradoxes of her personality, bleating through my consciousness.

The second day I tried a different strategy: I *only* sang "Hand in My Pocket." It didn't work, not really, but I felt I was on to something: as I wailed the words hoarsely into the small dark room—Alanis's litany of contradictory feelings, overwhelmed and high and hopeful and lost—they seemed to take on a deeper significance. They resonated like talismans of hidden meaning: like if I only sang them enough times, *in my own voice,* they would reveal their secrets, and I would be cured, enlightened, released from the torture of their repetition.

· · ·

For the past couple of years, I'd had exactly two feelings: "overworked" and "content." Dennis and I put in twelve- to fourteen-hour days at the firm, and then we got take- out, had quick sloppy sex on one padded piece of furni- ture or another, and conked out while looking through condo listings, waking up the next morning with the iPad sleeping between us like a baby.

Dennis is not the kind of man I would previously have imagined myself marrying. He is twelve years older than me and has a receding hairline and speaks loudly, like a game-show host. When I was younger, I'd imagined my- self with the kind of man I'd always dated—the kind who spoke softly and wore faded concert T-shirts and consid- ered himself a feminist and wanted to be a social worker or a public defender. My former boyfriends, collectively, would have disdained Dennis. I know the word they would have used. That word is "douche." They would have used this word—which technically refers to a clean- ing implement for women's vaginas, and therefore, when you think about it, is not a word that should be used by genuinely feminist men as an insult—to signify Dennis's embrace of corporate culture, his lack of shame.

But here's the thing: all the qualities those boyfriends claimed to embody, Dennis actually *did*. He was kind. He was a caring, respectful partner. He was honest too: he didn't pretend to care more about justice or honor than about food or money. And paradoxically, because his own needs were more than satisfied in the food-and-money department, he could afford to meet the world with benevolence. I saw the vigor with which he attacked his pro bono cases: helping a trafficked Serbian immigrant gain asylum, taking down an uptown molecular-gastronomy restaurant that owed its workers months of back pay. Sure, for every evil restaurant owner he took down, there was an evil corporation he propped up. Yet I couldn't say that he did any less good, overall, than my sour, embattled exes, shepherding their indigent clients in circles through the Kafkaesque bureaucracies of government aid programs. What moral life *wasn't* Sisyphean, tilted toward failure as much as success? The best one could do, it seemed, was to accept that paradox and try to really fucking enjoy oneself in the breaks between pushing the rock uphill.

I sang "Hand in My Pocket" a total of nineteen times (I counted). Again I had the feeling of asymptotically approaching their meaning, but that meaning remained shrouded, veiled in mystery. What was the significance, anyway, of the song's refrain? What was *one hand in my pocket* meant to suggest? To explore this question I tried it myself. I slid my hand into my own pocket while singing the words. Or tried to. But the pants I was wearing—form-fitting cigarette pants from Brooklyn Industries, just formal enough to pass as corporate—

turned out to have no real pockets, just little seamed slits meant to resemble them. Cosmetic pockets.

For some reason, this discovery annoyed me. More than annoyed me: it filled me with rage. I don't know why. I also don't know why my response to this rage was to jam my hand right into the fake pocket, hard, as I belted out the final chorus: "'Cause I've got one hand in my pocket, and the other one is hailing a taxicab!"

Because I was singing at the top of my lungs, I felt the rip rather than heard it. That quick jab of my hand had somehow torn the entire right-hand front panel of the pants away from the back, exposing the front of my thigh. A flap of cloth hung down like a lolling tongue. In the weird light of the karaoke room, my exposed flesh looked sickly and whorish, pale green and mottled by swirling disco lights.

"Motherfucking Brooklyn Industries," I murmured, dropping the microphone onto the vinyl couch with a muffled thud.

I hunted through my purse, but it contained nothing helpful: no spare clothing, no safety pins, no adhesive tape, not even a Band-Aid. It was a warm early-fall day, and I didn't even have a blazer or cardigan I could tie around myself to hide the hole. I had two options: call Dennis and tell him where I was so that he could bring me a new pair of pants, or go out into the world like this, holding my purse in front of me to conceal the torn fabric as best I could.

AMY BONNAFFONS

The choice wasn't really a choice. Just the thought of telling Dennis where I was filled me with a hot rush of shame. How would I explain it? How would he respond to this evidence of a craziness I hadn't previously displayed? ("You know what I love about you?" he'd once said. "You're sexy, but you're also *reasonable*.") I held the flap of cloth close to my skin with one hand, pulled the purse against it with the other, and hobbled out of JoyfulSongTime.

Luckily, there was a Gap right across the street. I limped inside and hunted through the rack of black pants. I quickly tried a pair, ascertained that the fit and style were similar enough, and wore them out, tossing my old pants into a garbage can on the street. As I walked the twelve blocks back to work—now almost late for a meeting with the senior partner—I slid my hands into the pockets of the new pants. Real pockets. The song was still blaring through my head, Alanis's unmistakable nasal voice piercing my consciousness, and there was something oddly comforting about being able to enact its lyrics directly. I left one hand in my pocket the whole way back to work.

Dennis had no children with his ex-wife. Which is, you know, thank God, right? I thought it might be nice to become a mother someday, a mother to something that began as a formless pink blob inside my body—but I couldn't imagine becoming an instant mother to a fully formed human child, with preexisting allegiances to another woman who hated me.

When I'd asked him if Carlene had wanted kids, he'd shrugged and said, "Let's not talk about that, okay? I want them with *you*." I tried not to think about the implications of his answer. I tried not to feel as if I'd stolen another woman's future children.

Carlene was thirty-nine now, not technically too old to become a mother, but old enough to panic about it. I thought I'd seen that panic in her eyes the day we'd first met, at the firm's Christmas party, before Dennis and I had technically started boning but well into the period when it was clear we eventually would. We were fucking constantly with our eyes, and it was obvious the rest of our bodies would soon follow. There was a palpable uneasy excitement stretched between us at all times, even when we were at opposite ends of the room; when we stood next to each other it collapsed, tightly coiled, into a pulse of sexual energy so thick it short-circuited and stalled conversations. Carlene was wearing a lime-green dress that hugged her Irish curves, and her thick red hair spilled down onto her shoulders. She was an objectively sexy woman. Yet here she might as well have been a medieval eunuch. She compensated by being aggressively friendly to me, stretching her fleshy lips into a strained, overly large smile and saying "That's so *great!*" to every innocuous fact I revealed about my life: what college I had attended, what neighborhood I lived in, what particular fitness classes I enjoyed. She sensed that she was on a sinking ship, and wanted to go down with her head held high. I respected her for that. Until I ran into her one day at Starbucks nine months later and she dumped what was left of her latte onto my shoes and said "This is *my* Starbucks, you ferret-faced cunt." (Unbeknownst to me, she and Dennis had carved up the city during their breakup, splitting custody of it as if it were the child they'd never had. They each had spheres of influence, where the other could not trespass: Carlene had all the Starbucks south of Thirty-Fourth Street and all Equinox gyms; Dennis had Fairway.)

Walking back from JoyfulSongTime in my new pants, an insane thought occurred to me: *I have been cursed.* That was a thing in some cultures, right? That one woman could curse another—that her hatred could become strong enough to infiltrate her rival's consciousness, perhaps even her womb? Was it Carlene's voice I was hearing in my head now, blaring out these stupid lyrics, causing me to rip my own pants? Was it Carlene's rage that had swept my uterus clean of whatever might have been nurtured there?

I shook my head. I was going bonkers. I pushed the revolving door and strode through the lobby, putting on my game face for my meeting, remembering what I was here for: I was here to defend Bank of America from external litigation, and I was here to make money doing it, and to look damn *good* while doing it, and you know what, *fuck* Carlene—if Dennis hadn't wanted to be with her anymore, there was nothing I could have done about it. Some forces are just impossible to fight.

Not that I had tried.

That night, while I stood at the kitchen counter pouring us each a glass of Pinot, Dennis came up behind me and slid his hands into my back pockets, cupping my ass. "Hmm," he said. "I like this. Wait, are these new?"

"No!" I cried, a little bit too loudly—so loudly that I startled myself and spilled the wine all over the granite countertop. "Oops," I said, leaning away from Dennis to reach for a paper towel.

"Really?" he said. "I'm sure I haven't seen these before. I'm sure because I notice your ass. I spend a lot of time noticing your ass. Full disclosure."

"I don't wear them a lot," I said, laying paper towels on the spill, watching them bloom blood-red. "They're old."

"Well, you should wear them more often," he said, turning me around to face him and sliding his fingers down into the front pockets. This action filled me with an inexplicable panic, and I twisted away from him. "The thing is," I said, reaching for the two now-full glasses of wine and handing one to him, "I actually *hate* these pants." I was surprised by the way the word "hate" emerged from my mouth: I practically spat it out, with twisted vehemence. Softening, I rushed to explain: "It's just something about the material. It kind of itches."

Dennis's eyes widened. "Okay," he said, shrugging. "Then don't wear them. Your ass looks good in other things too. Your ass looks good in everything. Here." He set his wine down on the counter, without even taking a sip, and began to unbutton the pants. He nuzzled his lips into the crook of my neck and murmured into my ear. "If you hate these so much, let me help you out of them."

What kind of woman stands in the kitchen of her Upper West Side apartment, sipping from a glass of '97 Pinot while her handsome rich fiancé slides her pants down and begins to slowly, expertly eat her out, and finds herself distracted by a dumb midnineties song she doesn't even like?

'Cause I've got one hand in my pocket, and the other one is giving a high five.

It was too much, the cognitive dissonance of it. "You know what I was thinking?" I said, reaching down and lightly tugging on Dennis's ears to disengage his face from my crotch. "About the wedding. I know the caterers suggested that roast chicken. But, you know, chicken at weddings...I mean, have you ever had wedding chicken that was really *compelling*?"

He looked up at me, brow furrowed. "Compelling?" he said.

"Yeah."

"You're interrupting cunnilingus to discuss whether a piece of food you might eat in six months will be *compelling* enough?"

"I'm sorry," I said, pulling him up to his feet, leaning into him and planting a kiss on his neck. "I'm just in a weird mood today."

"What's up?"

"I don't know. Wedding planning, I guess."

He sighed. "Listen, Chris," he said. "I'm dying to marry you. But, and I hate to bring this up, but I've *been* through this before. I know what a wedding does and doesn't mean. I want it to be a fun party. I want you to be happy. But I really could care less about how compelling the chicken is."

"You mean you *couldn't* care less."

"What?"

"If you *could* care less, that means you *do* care. What you're trying to say is that you don't care at all."

"But that's what I said."

"Never mind." I sighed. "Do you mind if we just go to bed? I'm tired."

That night I dreamed I was being chased by some shadowy creature through the crowded streets of the city. It had no face, or discernible body parts; it seemed to be covered in some kind of fringe that flap-flap-flapped as it ran. I ran up Fifth Avenue, over to Columbus Circle, back down Seventh; as I turned left, toward my office, I could feel it drawing closer, its moist cottony breath against the back of my neck. I turned and saw what the "fringe" was: the monster was made up of hundreds—possibly thousands—of pockets, covering every inch of

AMY BONNAFFONS

its surface, all turned inside out, flapping sadly against its side like used condoms.

"This is what happens," said the monster, in Carlene's voice, "when you turn yourself inside out."

I screamed again, and my scream woke me up.

The song was still blaring through my brain, louder than ever.

That day, on my lunch break, I did not go to Joyful-SongTime. Instead, I walked downtown, to the elementary school near Gramercy Park where I knew that Carlene taught fourth grade, and sat on a bench outside the fenced-in schoolyard. I nursed a large iced coffee and waited, though I wasn't sure exactly what for.

The children playing in the schoolyard all looked Nordic and robust and well cared for, dressed in snug fall jackets and brightly colored sneakers, whooping and cackling and running in circles. About 75 percent of them were blond. I could just imagine them, these children's blond mothers, prancing down the sidewalks like thoroughbreds in their Lululemon yoga pants, their bodies bearing no marks of childbirth (perhaps some of them having even avoided the ordeal entirely by transplanting their blond eggs into some brown woman's body), still trophy wives long into their supposed middle age, when they'd send their blond children off to elite blond universities with a faint blond wave.

After fifteen minutes, I'd finished my iced coffee and

was considering getting up to leave—what was I *doing* here, anyway?—when she emerged from the side door of the school, leading her own class out into the schoolyard: Carlene, her long red hair swept up into an elegant twist at the back of her head, wearing a pretty dark-green sweater-dress and excellent brown leather boots, her hand on her belly.

She looked about six months pregnant.

I needed to leave, but I couldn't bring myself to get up. For the moment, my head was thunderously silent: no song, no internal monologue, just the pounding of my blood and the pulse of one monosyllabic question: *how?*

I sat there watching, unable to even think about moving, unable to think about anything. I just watched Carlene, transfixed. She shepherded the line of children out into the schoolyard and then set them free, walking over to join the group of teachers chatting and patrolling from the sidelines. I watched her laughing, making conversation with the other teachers, periodically resting a proprietary hand on her stomach or leaning down to respond to the question of a child tugging on her dress. She looked radiant, like an exceptionally well-dressed Earth Mother, not anything at all like the sour, embittered woman who'd dumped a latte onto my shoes a year earlier.

Yet when she turned in my direction, I couldn't help myself: I got up and fled, walking away as fast as I could, before she might recognize me. Meanwhile the song started up in my head again, loud as ever.

"I was just wondering," I asked Dennis, later—we were on the couch, about to dig into a takeout artisanal pizza strewn with artichokes and arugula, then turn on *The Daily Show*—"have you heard from Carlene lately?"

"No. Why would I have heard from Carlene?"

"I don't know. I was just wondering about her for some reason."

"Why?"

"I just, you know—I guess I feel *bad* about it sometimes."

"So do I." He frowned, for just a second, before his face rippled back into its usual expression of masculine serenity. He shrugged. "But what can you do? We weren't happy. We hadn't been happy for a long time. And then I met you."

"Do you think she'll get married again?"

"I hope so." He sighed. "You remember, I had coffee with her when you and I got engaged—I didn't want her to hear it from someone else. She seemed fine. Took it well. I didn't get the sense she was with anyone, though."

It seemed impossible that Dennis would not have heard of Carlene's pregnancy, but if he had, he had no reason not to share it with me. I had to conclude that he genuinely didn't know. This made me feel slightly crazier, as if I'd imagined the pregnancy, or as if it somehow existed for my eyes only.

Why didn't I tell him what I'd seen? Would it have cost me anything? Maybe not, but somehow I couldn't think of a way to bring it up without explaining the whole train of insane logic that had led me to the bench from which I'd observed his ex-wife—the song, the possible miscarriage, my crazy idea of a curse. None of it made sense to *me*; how could I explain it to another person, even to him?

Especially to him. Dennis was so passionately logical. That was one of the things that had initially impressed me about him. He loved to argue, but not in the blustery overblown way that many men do; he'd listen to your argument, nodding with deep comprehension, making you feel that you'd never been more closely listened to in your life. Then he would pronounce one sentence, with the cadence of an announcement, and the coolness of its refrigerator-crisp logic would make everything else fall away; it was like taking a shower at the gym next to a model-thin woman and suddenly becoming aware of your own flab, *qua* flab. Initially, when I first met him as a summer associate, this quality of Dennis's had intimidated me, made me feel wobbly and diffuse. But then it took on a sexual edge; it was a turn-on for both of us when he demolished me like that. I was a very smart person, I was a good lawyer, but next to Dennis my own way of thinking seemed intuitive, impressionistic, full of curves. It was oddly flattering to both of us when we argued, this sexualized inscription of difference. Yet lately, when he'd cut through some cellulitic worry of mine with the scalpel of his logic, I'd felt exposed, diminished, vaguely lonely. Why was there so much of me I had to explain? Why was there so *much* of me?

"How did you know?" I heard myself asking.

"Know what?"

"That you weren't happy. With Carlene."

"What do you mean, how did I know? If you're not happy, you're not happy."

"But you stayed with her for a while after that, right? After knowing?"

"I guess so. Sometimes it takes a while to fully admit to yourself that you know something. Or it takes something else coming along. Something better." He squeezed my thigh.

"And what if I hadn't come along? How would you have known then?"

He frowned. "What are you getting at?"

"I'm not getting at anything. I'm just curious."

"Don't be curious," he said, leaning over and kissing my neck. "Just be happy. *I'm* happy." His hand was still on my thigh; now he slid it up further. I thought of the moment in the karaoke room when my pants had ripped, when my thigh had been exposed to the swirling greenish disco lights. It was this part of my thigh he was touching now. I was suddenly saturated with a self-disgust so thick that I actually gagged. "I don't feel so good," I said. "I think I might just go to bed."

"What about the pizza?"

I looked longingly at the box, steaming fragrantly on the coffee table in front of us, not yet opened. Its tomatoey, herbed aroma filled up the room. I wanted it, but not as badly as I wanted to be alone. "I think it might make me barf," I said. "I'm just gonna go lie down."

"What's going on with you?"

"Nothing. I just don't feel well. Stress, maybe. The change of season."

He smiled. "You're not pregnant, are you?"

"Of course not! Dennis, I just got my period, don't you remember? I went home from work. You gave me a back rub that night."

"Calm down," he said. "Of course I remember. I'm joking."

"Don't joke about that, please."

He held up both palms. "Sorry. I guess you *should* go to bed."

"I'm going."

From the darkness of our bedroom I could still smell the pizza, could hear the TV crowd's muffled laughter, could sometimes even hear Dennis laughing along with them, as if everything were just fine. It was odd, experiencing this all from the outside: hearing the sounds of our life, smelling its smells, without participating. Was this what my life would be like, without me?

• • •

The next day I went back to the elementary school again. I sat on the same bench, sipped an iced coffee from the same Starbucks, waited again for Carlene to emerge.

She did, at the same time as she had the day before: today in nicely tailored dark jeans and a kind of maternity peasant blouse, her red hair down around her shoulders. I strained to glimpse the presence or absence of a wedding ring, but I was too far away.

As I had the day before, I watched her walk over to the group of teachers, chatting while keeping an eye on the children's antics. I wasn't sure what I was waiting for, what I had hoped to see, beyond confirming the truth of what I'd observed yesterday. I was just about to get up and leave when she turned in my direction—then paused, squinted, and stiffened in recognition.

I raised a hand weakly in greeting. She murmured something to the teacher next to her, let herself out the gate in the chain-link fence, and strode over to the bench where I was sitting. She looked down at me, hands on hips, as if I were one of her errant students. But she didn't exactly look hostile: more like wearily patient, as if she'd been expecting this moment for a long time.

"I was just in the neighborhood," I said. "I didn't know you worked here."

She sat down next to me, arranging herself on the bench, resting a hand lightly on her belly. "Somehow," she said, looking straight ahead, "I find that hard to believe."

"You look...great."

"Thanks," she said, turning to face me, with a smile so large it must have been involuntary and genuine. "I've always wanted kids. And so when, you know—I thought, fuck it. I'll do it on my own. And I have to say, it's *already* the best choice I've ever made, and I haven't even met the baby yet."

Usually, when pregnant women say that they're excited to "meet" their babies, I want to vom. As if the baby is already this fully formed person with opinions and a personality, who they'll *finally* get to sit down and have coffee with. When my sister's was born, we all made this big fuss about the arrival of a new person, and then the new person turned out to be not a person at all but a wrinkled, larval sac of bodily fluids. There was nothing *to* "meet." Yet when I heard Carlene use the phrase, I felt oddly touched. I could tell she really *meant* it, not as a smug pregnant-woman platitude but as an actual description of her feelings.

"Everybody's rallying around me," she continued. "I have more support than I would have if I'd stayed married to Dennis. Dennis was never home for more than five minutes. You know?"

I did know. That morning, when I'd awoken at six-thirty, he was already gone. He liked to get to the office before anyone else. He was one of those people who barely rest, who view the need for sleep as a faintly pitiable quirk.

"That's great," I said weakly. "I'm happy for you." I was surprised and oddly disappointed, hearing the words come out of my mouth, to realize that they were true, or at least *could* be true. I could suddenly see Carlene in a detached, disinterested way; we had nothing to do with each other. I might have stolen her husband once, but what difference did that make, now? She was happy. I hadn't stolen her future babies, and she hadn't stolen mine. Even if such a thing were possible, she had no reason to curse me.

Realizing this, I should have felt free, but instead I felt weighed down more heavily than ever. Because, if the psychic explanation for my malaise did not involve Carlene, whatever *thing* was attacking me had come from some other place: some place that was harder to define, harder to assign a location outside of myself.

"Thanks," said Carlene. She frowned again. "So why *are* you here?"

"I don't know," I said. "I honestly don't." I stood up. "I have to run," I said. "They need me back at work. I've got a meeting in half an hour."

"Okay, but—"

I didn't hear Carlene finish her sentence, because I was already walking away.

I did not walk back to work, though. I hadn't been lying about the meeting, but I just couldn't go back there right now. I couldn't be around all those people who thought I was this one thing when I felt like this other thing. Something was pounding through my head, an almost unbearable pressure, something independent of the song, though the song was still there too, now starting to skip like a broken record: *'Cause I've got one hand in my pocket, and the other one, the other one, the other one...*

I went back to JoyfulSongTime, paid the teenage attendant, accepted the sparkly tambourine. But when I finally found myself alone in room 6, I didn't pick up the remote and punch in a number. Instead I just pulled my knees in close to my chest, rested my forehead on them, and began to sob.

A karaoke room in the middle of the day is a great place to cry, because you can be completely alone. It's the last place anyone would expect to find you. Even if I'd been home, I would have felt more exposed, among all the objects that used to be my own and which I now shared with Dennis, intermingled with the objects that had once been his and Carlene's, and the objects we had purchased together. Here in room 6 there was nothing personal, only binders full of songs cataloging the variable and yet endlessly predictable permutations of human feeling. Here my privacy was the most common, clichéd thing in the world. Here I could safely turn myself inside out.

I cried for half an hour straight, and then my Black-Berry started to buzz. It was Dennis. I was late for the meeting, of course. I let it buzz until it died, and then it started buzzing again. Then a text came through: *Chris are you OK?? I'm worried about you. Fuck the meeting. Just tell me where you are.*

I hit the reply button, then stared down helplessly at the device. Was it even possible to tell him where I was? Where *was* I?

When Dennis found me, I was lying supine on the long padded couch in room 6, my hands at my sides, like a corpse. I wasn't crying anymore. I was staring up at the ceiling, at the swirling pattern of lights that spangled its surface; yet my focus lay elsewhere, on something beyond the visible.

What I was focused on was the silence. When I had finally stopped crying, my head was blindingly clear, like a landscape blanketed in snow. The song was gone. *Everything* was gone—except this silence, like a taut tightrope across which I now had to navigate without losing my footing. I couldn't be distracted. I felt a clarity that was wordless, without reference. It had no message. It *was* the message: a tight humming blankness that belonged to me, that demanded my attention, that demanded everything.

I heard the door open. I heard Dennis come in. I heard him speak my name. I did not reply, or turn my head to acknowledge him.

I knew that I would have to speak soon, that I would have to tell him some things. What I didn't yet know, what I hoped that the silence would reveal to me, was just how many things there were. And also: would he be able to hold these things, to cup them in his palms and accept them—or would he hand them back to me, impenetrable as mirrors, mine and mine alone?

He sat down next to me, his expensively suited butt squeaking on the cheap vinyl as he settled himself. He said nothing. He took both of my hands into both of his. I tried to pull them away, but he held them tighter. Then he looked up at the ceiling, where I was looking, and waited for me to speak: so patiently that it was like he wasn't waiting at all, like he was simply watching the miasmic patterns of the disco lights as if they held great interest, sanguine about whatever mysteries or banalities they might reveal.

I opened my mouth and heard myself begin to speak. The sentence I spoke was not the one I had planned. What I said was "I've lost something."

"What?" said Dennis, gently. "What do you mean, baby? What have you lost?"

I had no idea how to begin.

Horse

Every morning we meet in the kitchen and unsheathe our needles. Serena delicately peels down her underwear, exposing a modest triangle of buttock; I count to three, hold her hip to steady her trembling frame, then jab, thrusting the handle until the fluid disappears. She exhales, in one quick hiss, like a cat. Then I turn and bend over, underwear around my ankles. I don't care what she sees: my cottage-cheese ass, the tuft of fur between my legs. I used to wax and prune, to spread "smoothing creams" on every inch of my body, even the parts no one ever saw in the daylight—but since I started taking the shots, my attitude has changed.

Needles don't scare me like they do Serena. But when she plunges it in, I give a little yelp of solidarity. We are in this together—at least for now.

The two needles look identical, although their contents are different. We have different goals. Serena wants to become a mother. I want to become a horse.

Q: *What does it mean to be a horse?*

A: *First, it means not being a person. No credit cards, no fad diets, no existential questions, no more boring meetings or family dinners. No political allegiances or disappointments, no responsibility to anyone but yourself. Mostly: no embarrassment, which (as a great writer once said) is the fundamental condition of being human.*

Q: *How do I become one?*

A: *It's quite simple. State your desire in writing and we'll take it from there.*

Q: *Is it expensive?*

A: *No.*

Q: *Why not?*

A: *Because there is not yet sufficient demand for the procedure. All the more reason for you to try before it becomes pricey and exclusive. Right now it costs less than a Pi-*

*lates vacation in Tulum. Would you rather transform
your core, or your entire being?*

Every time she saw the blue minus sign, she said, Serena heard a big game-show buzzer going off inside her head. She was running out of time: only one more round of IVF before her money dried up. In the meantime, her ovaries swelled painfully, she felt like a hormone-soaked sponge. I didn't say so—I held her hand, I told her she was beautiful and perfect, I spoke soothing words about the future—but she *looked* like a hormone-soaked sponge: bloated, leaking feeble aimless tears.

Serena's name fit her perfectly: she was sleek, composed, never a hair or a word out of place. Even in rare moments of rage, or grief, or drunkenness, she seemed exquisitely self-controlled; her emotions seeped out of her like an invisible vapor, leaving her porcelain-doll face, her slim body, unchanged. Now, though, she'd begun to grow blurry. This was what she wanted, to blur and smudge her own outlines: but she wanted pregnancy, not anxiety or disappointment, to be the cause.

Meanwhile, I felt my formerly messy self congeal, cohere, grow tight and purposeful; I became leaner, more alert. Sometimes, walking down the street, I gave my long hair a toss, I almost let out a whinny of delight.

Q: How does the process work?

A: The process now known as Equinification was discovered
by Dr. Janus Beláček, a Hungarian doctor employed by
the government of Croatia. While using horse DNA to
test a method of improving hair luster, Beláček discovered that his subjects—but only the females—had begun
to grow hooves. This accidental discovery enabled
Beláček to extend his formula, transforming human
DNA into horse DNA. The process requires only a simple series of shots.

Q: Where do these horse-women live?

A: Atalanta Ranch, which occupies an entire island off the
coast of Florida and has been built expressly for this purpose.

Q: What do the horses on the ranch look like?

A: They look like horses, which is to say that they look exactly
like themselves: tall graceful animals designed for running and for grazing, muscles rippling beneath a shiny
coat of fur, hair flying in the wind. They don't look like
the sad, compromised horses you might see plodding
around muddy rings carrying children, or dragging
tourist-laden carriages through a city park. They look

like they are doing nothing other than actively being themselves—as if this, the act of being themselves, joyfully absorbs all of their attention. They lap from clear pools beneath waterfalls, they canter across open fields, they nibble grass at the base of exquisite, tree-lined foothills.

Q: Are the horses happy?

A: There is no way of knowing for sure.

Q: But what's your gut feeling, though?

A: How could something that beautiful not be happy?

"Why do you want to be a mom so bad, anyway?" I asked Serena. We sat across from each other at the kitchen table, fingers curled around steaming mugs of tea, the offending pee-stick faceup between us. "It's weird that I've never asked you."

"I don't know," she said. "I just always have."

"Are you sure you *really* want it? That it's not, you know, just socialization?"

She set her mug down and closed her eyes, as if gathering her thoughts, and then opened them. "Sometimes I want to hold a baby so badly," she said, curving her arms around the invisible burden, "and it's not an idea, it's a physical need. It's stronger than the need for sex.

AMY BONNAFFONS

The warmth, the weight—I don't know. It's incredibly specific. It's a more specific desire than I've ever felt for any man." She looked at me. "You've never felt that, not even a little bit?"

I shook my head. "And I've always thought, when people say they want to start a family, why would anyone want to create *more family*? Isn't family the thing we're all trying to get away from?" She laughed, while I blushed and backpedaled: "I mean, yours won't be like that. Yours will be great."

She shrugged. "My kid won't always like me. Maybe I won't even like him or her all the time. But I don't care. It's like—" She hesitated for a moment. "You're going to think this is cheesy, but I heard this song lyric once that described children as 'life's longing for itself.' That's the best way I can describe it."

I blinked, startled by the phrase. "I know exactly what that means," I said. "Life's longing for itself. But for me, it has nothing to do with children."

Serena had a husband once: Bill. Nothing was wrong with him, really; he just didn't stick. Some people slide right off each other, despite their best attempts to stay attached.

I've never had a husband, or a wife. I've had lovers, some briefly, some for ages. One of us always left. At first I thought I was failing at something and then I realized I was aiming for the incorrect goal. In trying to knit my life together with someone else's, I was going in the wrong direction entirely: what I wanted was to be free, utterly free.

At first love appeared to offer freedom; it gave me a kind of soaring feeling, the world seemed to belong especially to me. But every long-term arrangement made a mockery of this initial flight: each shared domestic situation became a sadistically nurtured garden of resentments, each nonmonogamous configuration required a volume of careful politics—of unceasing demands disguised as negotiations—that I imagine it might take to run a progressive, moderately sized nation. Sweden, for example.

But single life didn't offer the kind of freedom I wanted, either, with its stale routines, its clumsy infrequent sex. What I wanted was something not offered by human existence at all: the wild, unfettered life of the body. As I neared my fortieth birthday, I felt increasingly constricted by daily postures—sitting in a chair at my desk; hunched over the steering wheel in my car; cocking my head with feigned interest at a party; stirring spaghetti sauce over the stove. I started taking expensive vacations to engage in extreme physical challenges: mountain climbing, skydiving, snowboarding. These pursuits all induced a feeling of mastery and freedom, but only after learning a complex set of rules regarding harnesses, buckles, and straps. I wanted to do away with constraints entirely.

Then I learned about the ranch.

Q: Does the process always work?

A: Unfortunately, no.

Q: What are the potential side effects?

A: Sterility, seizures, Centaurism.

Q: Why does it only work on women?

A: We're not sure, but we think it's because they want it to.

Q: Is that how science works?

A: No one understands how science works, not even the most
   scientific scientists. Dr. Beláček himself has been given
   to grand pronouncements of the following nature: "It's
   desire, not gravity, that holds the universe together—
   and desire, not dark energy, that pulls it apart. Out-
   comes do not respond to our efforts in a linear way;
   rather, outcomes retroactively reveal the depth and mys-
   tery of our desires. My process is nothing more, or less,
   than a patented conundrum."

Q: What does that mean?

A: It's hard to say without a working knowledge of Hungarian

idiomatic expressions. In the obscure dialect region from
which Dr. Beláček comes, the same word is used for "co-
nundrum," "miracle," and "mistake"; it has also been
used to refer to the feathers of a chicken (but only in cir-
cumstances when they are no longer attached to the
chicken).

Of course, I went to visit. Otherwise, how could I be certain it wasn't a scam? Serena had been skeptical from the beginning: "I don't know, Cass," she said. "What if there *is* no ranch, and it's all some plot to turn gullible women into pack animals? What if it's some awful military-industrial-complex type of thing?"

But the ranch was just as they'd described. The horses looked healthy and vibrant. Conspiracy theories like Serena's had been debunked by that point anyway—journalists from all the major news organs had thrown up their hands, finding no evidence of a sinister agenda—but there was nothing like seeing it for myself. Their hooves pounding across the plains, making a sound like rainfall; their coarse hair rippling in the wind; their quiet gaze of recognition as they watched us approach.

"Do you think this is some kind of modern version of the lesbian separatist utopia?" I mused that night to Cathy, one of the other women on the tour, over gin and tonics at the island's guesthouse. "Except not just for lesbians."

She laughed. "Old fantasies die hard." She gave me

a meaningful look. "Can I ask something? What's your reason?"

"Boredom," I said, without hesitation.

She nodded; my answer seemed to make sense to her. "What about you?" I said. "What are you escaping?"

She replied with a long story about her body, which had endured nearly every tried-and-true form of female trauma: abuse, rape, abortion, endometriosis, hysterectomy. "I guess," she said, "I want a different body, with a clean slate."

They kept refilling our drinks, without our asking, and soon we were very drunk. Somehow we found ourselves in my room, stripping off our clothes, hungrily tonguing and sucking each other's bodies as if, by taking in the other's flesh, we could achieve the kind of transcendence we were hoping for, while still remaining human. This sex was like a competition: who could manage to escape her body, using the other's body, first? We pushed against each other with such violence that orgasm became inevitable. But the noise she emitted as she came—a helpless whimper, like a child's—brought me back into the room. Embarrassed by what her cry had introduced, we turned away from each other. Just then, I sensed movement behind the window; boldly I got up, stark naked, and pulled aside the curtain. One of the horses was standing right outside, staring in with her dark liquid eyes. I felt the bed creak behind me, then heard Cathy gasp: so she saw it too. The horse gave a deep, slow nod, as if to demonstrate that we had understood each other; then she turned and disappeared into the night.

Q: When I become a horse, will I still have human consciousness?

A: We believe this question is best answered by iconoclastic seventeenth-century Jewish philosopher Baruch Spinoza, who tragically died from the effects of inhaling glass dust. Spinoza defines God in the following way: "By God I mean an absolutely infinite being, that is, a substance consisting of infinite attributes, each of which expresses eternal and infinite essence." In other words, a horse and a woman and a stone are not different things, but rather all attributes of the same thing, which is God. "Every substance is necessarily infinite," Spinoza writes, but has its own "essence." In a similar manner, you will simultaneously be your human self and not be your human self when you become a horse. You will think the same thoughts, but in a horsey manner; your personality will have the same attributes, but horsily expressed; your thoughts will take on a horsey cadence, your feelings will pulse and throb with thick horsey blood. We cannot guarantee that you will continue to inhabit your human identity in any recognizable way. But much as Spinoza accepted that not only his human *lungs but also the glass that subtly punctured them and the air that suspended and delivered the glass to his pulmonary tissues were all made of the same substance—God—and that therefore his death was only a matter of taking God into God, of God puncturing God and delivering God into another form of God, we hope that you will accept any change in your nature as both natural and sacred, however artificially induced.*

Q: Do you believe in God?

A: No.

Serena went to the doctor, reported that the second attempt had failed. "We don't say 'failed,'" said the doctor, kindly. "We say 'unsuccessful.'"

"That's almost as bad," said Serena.

The doctor shrugged. "You want to have a baby," she said. "You should probably get used to feeling unsuccessful. It's not possible to 'succeed' at parenthood the way you've 'succeeded' in your career. Treating parenthood like a career can cause anxiety, wrinkles, and helicopterism, especially in older mothers like yourself. Sometimes I give my patients a mantra to repeat. *I will not succeed. I will not succeed.*"

"Oh," said Serena. Then, after a pause: "I wouldn't say I've succeeded in my career."

"I don't know anything about your career," said the doctor. "I was just using that as an example."

"Oh. Okay."

Serena is naturally self-deprecating; I, at least, consider her successful. We became friends in a Ph.D. program that she actually finished. I dropped out after our third year, when I realized that the most pleasurable part of my life was my summer waitressing job. At that job I felt competent, dexterous, sexy, a person who could face the world with an air of cockeyed challenge. I strutted between the kitchen and the dining room with plates expertly balanced on my forearms; I joked and flirted with the customers; I swore good-naturedly at the line cooks; I finished each shift pleasantly exhausted, my ponytail loosened by exertion and my body aching for earned indulgence. My nights often ended on the incense-scented mattress of another server, a drummer named Matty, where we fucked and smoked and fell asleep after four in the morning. When I had a day off, I spent it walking through the city, or going swimming or rock climbing, or reading books I actually wanted to read. It was an absorbing existence, and I didn't care that I might be atrophying the higher parts of my brain; for once, it seemed I had discovered something actually true about myself, not something that was just supposed to be true.

But it got old. Eventually I became annoyed at Matty—his generic compliments, his bad toenails, his constant quotation of *Zen and the Art of Motorcycle Maintenance*—and we got a meaner boss, and I started to get

AMY BONNAFFONS

a persistent pain in my hip that turned out to be sciatica. I tried a few other restaurant jobs, then finally settled for freelance copyediting, for which my half-degree apparently qualified me. I had no desire to go back to school— I just couldn't bring myself to believe that the world would ever care what I had to say about Virginia Woolf or Deleuze or anything, really, and anyhow I couldn't bring myself to care enough to say it.

Serena graduated with honors, and won an award for her thesis on eighteenth-century women's novels. For her, intellectual labor felt like labor, in a good way, the way waitressing had for me: honest and exhausting and satisfying. But after graduation, despite her accolades, she couldn't find a job. She had dozens of interviews, almost got several tenure-track positions, but in the end they always went with someone else. I encouraged her, but privately ascribed her failure to her meekness with strangers; with friends she was self-possessed, often cuttingly funny, but she was a cipher in interviews. She seemed to equate "professionalism" with a total erasure of her personality. In the end, after a few miserable years of adjuncting, she got a job teaching English at an all-girls high school. To her surprise, the girls recognized her quiet power and obeyed her, surrounded her with a mute halo of reverence. She became one of the school's most beloved teachers, supervising the literary club and an adorable baby-feminist zine, matter-of-factly explaining the mechanisms of birth control and orgasm to anyone too shy to ask the health teacher. Yet, no matter how deeply the work absorbed her, she always felt like a failure because she wasn't leading obscure seminars on object theory, or giving papers at the MLA conference, or being addressed as Professor Lowry. She suffered from crippling spasms of envy every time one of our former classmates got a job or published a paper. Eventually, after we became roommates, I forbade her from complaining; it seemed she was being ungrateful toward the gifts of her life. I was much worse off, bored and restless in a deeper, more fundamental way.

Yes, I was bored, I was deeply bored, I was rapidly approaching a crisis of boredom. It seemed more and more like boredom was the fundamental condition of my existence, a monolithic truth I ignored with less and less success as the years passed. I was bored with my job, bored with Boston, bored with my periodic escapes, bored with my attempts at relationships; by womanhood, personhood, life. I wondered whether I was *particularly* bored, or whether everyone secretly felt as I did and found ways to distract themselves. Either way, it was becoming intolerable.

Q: Isn't this really a glorified form of suicide?

A: We prefer to think of it in the opposite way, as a kind of birth: deliverance into a denser, quicker, more urgent form of life. But your friends, lovers, and relatives may not see it this way. You may have to prepare them for your transformation as you might for your death. Some choose to attend support groups with their friends and partners. Others complete their transformations in se-cret, leaving only a note behind.

Q: Will I need to make out a will, then?

A: Yes. You may not bring anything with you to Atalanta Ranch, besides your body.

Q: Can my loved ones visit?

A: Yes.

Q: Will they recognize me?

A: Most of them claim to, but it is impossible to determine how much this recognition depends upon wishful thinking.

Q: Can they ride me?

A: We don't recommend it. So far, every attempt has ended in tragedy.

It started happening right after my fortieth birthday, in June: I woke up in the middle of the night with a strange feeling in my feet—not pain, exactly, but pressure so intense it absorbed my whole attention. I cried out in surprise, and Serena rushed into my room, and then we pulled back the covers to see that my feet had been replaced by perfect horse hooves, black and stonelike.

As predicted by the pamphlets, I felt disgust, then wonder: *The transformation of your own body will be a spectacle arousing both revulsion and awe.*

I got up and tried to walk around. Serena and I both giggled, manically, the way terrified people do. My hooves were tender, and it hurt to walk on them, like when my feet used to ache at the end of a night on high heels. I felt lopsided and clumsy; these hooves weren't made to carry a bipedal organism. But hearing their *clop-clop-clop* around the floors of the apartment, I grew excited: it was really happening!

We couldn't sleep the rest of the night. We stayed up, rereading the informational pamphlets, speculating on how quickly the rest of me would start to turn. We had six months, we imagined, until the change spread up to my torso and I'd have to head down to the ranch to complete the rest of my transformation.

As if by magic, by some prearranged signal of the gods, Serena peed on another stick the next morning and discovered she was pregnant.

Q: Are the horses tame, or wild?

A: The horses at the ranch are wild. We provide nothing but acreage for running and grazing. We do nothing to "break" them. There are no harnesses, no bridles, no whips.

Q: What does it mean to break a horse?

A: A broken horse is an obedient horse. This obedience follows from trust, and from a system of rewards. The horse is habituated to its bridle, causing it to associate restraint with comfort. If done properly, restraint need not be a form of violence; rather, it is a language, a grammar of leather and human touch that the animal body comes to understand and to welcome. Yet we at Atalanta Ranch eschew human-imposed languages of any and all kinds. Among other purposes, the ranch exists in order to cultivate wildness.

Q: What is wildness? And may wildness be "cultivated," or is that phrase not oxymoronic?

A: That is what we're trying to find out. All we can say is: either you personally resonate with this desire, or you don't. Either you like the idea of shaking off your restraints, and are willing to give up everything you know in the attempt to do so, or you are like most people: comforted by language, by clothing, by laws.

Maybe you are the kind of woman who experiences this comfort but feels deeply suspicious of it, suspicious of all male inventions. Maybe you have longed to strip away the grammar of patriarchy and reinvent everything from the bottom up. If so, we welcome you, but with one important caveat: when you become a horse, you will not care about sisterhood or equity, and if you did, you would have no way of working toward these goals. Instead, most likely, you will care only about the kinesis of your muscles, the yellow butter of the sun, the furry grass between your powerful teeth.

Walking around town with my hooves, I gained a new kind of attention. Women regarded me with disgust or envy, men with disgust or desire. I'd heard, on my trip to the ranch, about people with Centauride fetishes, but I'd assumed it was a super-niche population—basically, people with a bestiality kink who'd discovered a new outlet. But it turned out to be a much wider spectrum.

My first night out at a bar with some friends, I was the object of many stares, but I sensed a particular heat coming from one man at a corner table. He wore the distinct, recognizable look of a graduate student: floppy hair and a lanky frame and a too-large cotton hoodie. He was at least thirty, but looked like he'd only recently learned how to dress himself. I kept feeling his gaze on the back of my neck. Every time I looked over at him, he turned away, red-faced. Eventually, when he approached the bar to get another drink, I addressed him.

"Hey," I said.

He blushed again, flicked his eyes down to my hooves, then back up, then blushed deeper. "Hey," he said.

"Am I the first you've seen?"

"Yeah," he said. "Sorry. I guess I was staring."

"It's OK."

"I'd heard about—you. But I wasn't sure it was real."

I shrugged. "Looks like it is."

"Is that—is that the only part of you that...?"

"So far, yes."

He nodded, swallowed, looked at me hungrily. I grabbed a pen from my purse, scribbled my number on a napkin. I wasn't particularly attracted to him, but I'd been hugely, aimlessly horny since my hooves had appeared.

"Look," I said, pushing the napkin toward him, "my friends and I are about to head to another bar—but if you want to meet up later, text me. I'll be free by midnight."

Later that night, on the mattress in his spartan studio apartment, he stared at my half-clad body as if he'd never seen a woman before. (Of course, he'd never seen one like *me*.) I felt his gaze playing over me, lingering on the spot where the slope of my ankle gave way to the ashen density of the hoof. The feeling reminded me of being with a boy for the very first time, in high school. He'd reached out for my breast with undisguised wonder; his desire had been enough to inflame my own.

Now, though, the hunger in the eyes of the floppy-haired grad student failed to make my general desire focus more specifically on him. Something was happening, though, a violent molten feeling welling up within me. As he reached out to touch me, to grasp me around the ankles, I recognized it as rage.

But it was too late: it had already happened. I had kicked him.

He jerked backwards, drawing his hands to his face. Blood seeped out between his fingers. He said something, or tried to, but all I heard was "unhh, *unhhh*."

The old me would have taken responsibility: would have gone and fetched him a towel, called a taxi, accompanied him to the hospital. But I was no longer human. The sight of his bloody face only increased my rage, tinged it with contempt for his weakness. I fought the urge to kick him again, harder; it was all I could do to get out of the house. I hurried down the stairs of his walk-up, pushed open the door, and ran through the streets of Somerville, awkward on my hooved limbs but propelled by the heat his near-touch had unleashed. It wasn't rage *at* anyone, or anything: just a pure, propulsive red-hot urge. I ran past Harvard's gates, over the bridge, through Boston at a full sprint. At some point I realized that my awkward gait had been replaced by something graceful and rhythmic and, well, horselike; I had stopped noticing the strangeness of my hooves, I was using them as they were meant to be used. I was cantering.

By the time I approached my own neighborhood, I'd slowed to a trot, but I felt elated: my very nature was changing. I was becoming wild. The man's touch had been a bridle, and I had kicked it away.

Q: *What symptoms might I experience during my transformation?*

A: *The same symptoms you would experience during any transformation: mood swings, growing pains, strained relationships. Also, possibly, the occasional blinding toothache. To find a Centauride support group near you, consult our website.*

Q: *Am I required to go to the ranch? Or can I make an arrangement in advance, in which a friend or relative agrees to take care of my horse-self on his or her own property?*

A: *This is permissible, albeit at a slightly higher cost (the cost of preparing the more complex legal paperwork that such an arrangement requires).*

Accept this caveat, though: your friend or relative must be aware of your wildness—of the fact that you most likely will not submit to their attempts at friendship, and if they persist, they may incur violence. If you are willing in advance to be domesticated by your friend/relative—to be "broken" by someone you love—

you must sign paperwork to that effect before completing your transformation.

Over the next few months, the change slowly inched upward. My human ankles became horse-ankles, I grew coarse caramel-colored hair on my legs, my femurs stretched and thickened. Occasionally I felt sharp pains in my bones—growing pains—but other than that, the physical transition felt invigorating.

My rage, however, only grew. I was energized by aimless, volcanic fury, 100 percent of the time. Perhaps I wasn't changing my nature but recognizing something that had always been there. My boredom had never really been boredom, but rather a deep, deep anger: the molten lava at the earth's core, unseen until it disrupts the placid surface.

Where had this come from? Did everyone have it? Or had I done too good a job of submitting to myriad invisible harnesses? Either way, it was obvious, now, to everyone I met. I responded to routine rudenesses—catcalling, crowding on the subway, an unsolicited hand on the shoulder—by snarling, flashing my eyes, baring my teeth. People's eyes grew wide; they stepped back; they treated me like the dangerous animal I was. I loved it.

Serena too was changing. Her first three months she'd looked sickly and drawn, she'd thrown up all the time, but finally the pregnancy had rooted in her body, and she blossomed. The first sonogram showed not one but two fetuses in her belly. Now her face looked inflated but ruddy, glowing with health. Every moment she wasn't teaching, she was at the computer, researching the development of the strange creatures inside of her.

I, on the other hand, found myself unable to sit still. I'd sit down, get through one paragraph, then feel it kick through me: the wildness, the aimless rage. I'd leave the house, drive to the river, canter up and down the path beside the Charles, kicking sod fiercely into the water until I got it out of my system. My white-hot anger was surrounded by a bright corona of joy: every act of violence rang in all my pleasure centers, sent a thrill of aliveness down my spine. This was what I'd been missing.

Then, one evening, I got so frustrated with my work that I stood up and kicked a hole right through the kitchen cabinet. This time, the joy was quickly eclipsed by horror: the splintered wood, the ugliness, the cost.

Serena appeared in the doorway, pale, one hand on the swell of her belly. We stared at each other, gripped by the same mute question: how much longer could we go on like this, sharing the same space—my destruction, her attempt to create?

That night, lying in bed, I heard the unmistakable sound of muffled weeping. I got up, knocked lightly on Serena's door, then cracked it open. At first she didn't notice me, because she was turned toward the wall. This gave me a moment to just look at her and feel my feelings.

I had two feelings, simultaneous but contradictory: a

rustling annoyance, the pitying contempt I'd come to feel for humans still trapped in their weak hairless bodies—but, also, compassion. Serena was the person who most reliably aroused my remaining human tenderness, and she was suffering. I walked in, sat on the edge of her bed, lightly stroked her hair. This only made her cry harder.

"What's the matter?" I asked.

"Nothing," she choked out. "Just hormones." But before I could respond, she corrected herself. "I'm fucking terrified. This is the biggest thing I've ever done. And I'm doing it totally alone."

"You won't be alone, you have your family. You have your friends."

She laughed bitterly. "Yeah. Except for you."

My brain flashed back on our ritual with the shots. That seemed like such a long time ago; the needles had done their work, we'd launched ourselves onto opposing trajectories. Did we still need each other? If not, did this mean we had failed to love each other, or that we had loved each other well?

With effort, Serena sat up in bed, wiped her eyes, looked at me. She was still waiting for me to respond.

I just stared at her. In the greenish light coming through the window, she seemed distinct and alien, like someone I had never seen, *really* seen, before. The protrusion of her belly was impossible to ignore: it crested just below her breasts, then stretched toward me, an insistent convexity with an agenda of its own. There were *two whole people* in there: for the first time, the terrifying marvel of this fact hit me full force. Perhaps her transformation was even stranger, even wilder, than mine.

"You can come visit me," I said. "Bring your kids to the ranch. It's so pretty there."

"And tell them what?"

"This is your aunt Cassie. She was restless, and she turned herself into an animal."

She snorted. "And what? That's supposed to be an example of some sort? Things get hard and you just leave? Just peace out of human life entirely?"

I shrugged. "Maybe it's a cautionary tale. This is what happens when you ignore your own wildness for too long. Your unhappiness becomes a second skin. You have to get an entirely different skin, in order to survive."

"You've really been that unhappy?"

"It hasn't been obvious?"

"I always thought you had so much more fun than me. You were constantly trying new things. You had none of my hang-ups about sex. You slept with men, you slept with women, you never seemed to care."

"Hm."

"Can I ask you something?"

"What?"

"Were you ever attracted to me?"

"To you?"

"Yes. Never mind. It's a stupid question."

"Were *you* attracted to *me*?"

"No, I don't think so. But there were times when I wished I was. That we could actually, like, *fuse* with each other. Like we could break into each other and both become something different."

"Yes," I said. "But maybe we *did* do that. Just not with sex. We're different now, aren't we?"

She considered this. "Then why am I so afraid?"

"I'm afraid too," I said. I'd spoken automatically, to comfort her, but as soon as I said it, I realized it was true.

We looked away from each other, toward the window—embarrassed as Cathy and I had been at the ranch, but for different reasons. This time, of course, no horse appeared: just a faint mist, illuminated by streetlights. What had been illuminated? Perhaps the wild thing in the room was not in fact my kicking legs, or the strange life inside of her, but what lay between us: the animal tide that can arise between two women, more mysterious than sex, hardly touched by the simple word "friendship." It rose and crested, it rocked the small bed like a lifeboat.

Q: Is the change reversible?

A: No change is ever reversible.

Q: What happens if the process doesn't work on me?

A: *You'll get your money back. We may ask you to participate in an ongoing scientific study of long-term Centauride health outcomes, for compensation—but you may decline.*

Q: **That's it?**

A: *It's not possible for us to do more. There are support groups; we can refer you to one in your area. However, your human or half-human life is out of our purview.*

Our legal agreement requires you to assume responsibility for the risk of the procedure's failure, before it begins; we try to make these risks clear. We ask this not only to protect ourselves from litigation, but to encourage each person considering the procedure to take responsibility for her own life in a way that should hopefully prove transformative, even if something goes wrong along the way.

This requires bravery. Our hope is that the Centaurides living among us will be viewed not as freaks or as failures, but as emblems of courage: female animals who gathered up all the uncertainties of their existence into one single, massive risk.

I went for a checkup with the Atalanta doctor. The visit was routine, had been scheduled for months, but I was nervous: my progress since the last visit seemed to have stalled. She examined me all over and said "Hmmm" a lot. I grew increasingly worried.

"When did you say the fur reached your belly button?" she asked.

"A month ago."

"And no change since then?"

"No."

"Hm."

"I don't like the sound of that 'hm.'"

"Well," she said, "the good news is that you're showing none of the other markers that usually accompany the procedure's failure. The bad news is, that means I have nothing to tell you about why this is happening, or whether it'll pick up again."

"So you think it's possible the procedure is failing?"

"It's possible."

"Shit."

"I'm sorry. I know this is stressful."

"Have you encountered this before? A case like mine?"

"Frankly, no." She smiled. "You're special."

"That's what my mom always said."

"We'll keep checking up on you. Don't lose heart. But in the meantime, you might want to make some arrangements for the next few months, in case you can't leave for the ranch as planned. Will that be a problem, do you think?"

It would be. The situation in our apartment was growing tense, nearly untenable: Serena was huge, growing huger by the day, while I stayed the same. I'd moved out of my bedroom—she needed it for a nursery—and given most of my possessions away. I was sleeping on the couch in the living room, unsure of how long I could stay.

The joy had gone out of my violence; it had become a compulsion, an irritating itch. I battled to restrain myself from destroying everything in the house. All day I ran along the river, roamed through town, pummeled punching bags at the gym, then arrived home at night to find Serena sulking like an abandoned cat. I'd stopped trying to explain why it was better for me to stay away.

But I wasn't avoiding her only out of concern for her, or her possessions: it was painful to witness the obviousness of her transformation, with my own now so uncertain.

When I got home from the doctor's, I saw that yet another delivery of baby stuff—hand-me-downs from friends, large Amazon boxes full of equipment—had arrived at the apartment, and completely taken over the living room. In other words, *my* room. To reach the couch, I had to pick my way over and between the boxes, stepping as delicately as possible with my horse-legs, legs that were not made to do anything delicately. Even when I got there, I couldn't sit down: it was piled high with baby clothes.

I lost it. I whirled around and began kicking with an aimless violence that, even after my run of rage-soaked months, startled me with its force. I had not intended this; I was beyond intention; I was fighting for my literal life, like if I stopped kicking and hurling things, I would implode into nothing, less than nothing, I would cease to exist.

By the time I'd managed to stop, I had wrecked not only most of the new baby equipment, but also the large flat-screen television and the coffee table; I had seriously damaged the couch. I looked around, at the torn baby blankets strewn with broken glass, the mutilated breast pump, the mangled stroller, the tiny books with their torn pages.

Just then, a key turned in the lock, and Serena stood in the doorway.

She looked from me to the mess, from the mess back to me. She didn't seem surprised, exactly; her perfect, masklike features did not move at all, but seemed to grow harder and sharper, to register a sudden sedimentation of dark knowledge.

It would be pointless to apologize. I could offer no defense or consolation. I only had one option.

"I'm going to leave now," I said. "I'll find someplace else to stay."

She nodded, with no expression, then walked into her bedroom and shut the door behind her. I picked up my purse and left.

I walked aimlessly, vaguely in the direction of the downtown hotels. My muscles grew leaden with shame. I felt like I was walking underwater.

What pained me was not the notion that my wildness, my horsiness, had finally overtaken me. It was the suspicion—the reluctant conviction—that my violence had been entirely human.

That night, under a scratchy hotel blanket, I contem-

AMY BONNAFFONS

plated my situation. While I was probably worse off now than I'd have been if I'd never attempted the transformation, in certain ways I had gotten exactly what I'd asked for. I'd received a revelation of my true nature. I had always been an awkward thing, stalled and half wild, willing to try anything but unable to commit, so suspicious of restraints that the suspicion itself became the biggest restraint of all.

For the first time in nearly a year, I cried: sobbing into the lumpy pillow, mourning the grotesque monster that I was, howling at my failure: my loneliness, my inadequacy as woman and as animal. Eventually, from sheer exhaustion, I slept.

When I woke in the morning, I saw that during my few hours of sleep the fur had finally reached upward. My breasts were gone, replaced by a fine equine torso. I raised my hands to touch it, then realized that they had been replaced by another set of hooves.

I wasn't stupid enough to think that this development had happened *because* of the previous night's revelations. Life is not like a self-help book, where you understand something about yourself and then the universe reaches out to physically manifest your new insight. We might long for change, work toward it with intention, but its arrival—if it ever arrives at all—always feels like an ambush.

Still, I was relieved. Maybe my horse-life wouldn't be

better; but it would be different. I would accept that difference humbly, allow it to work itself through me. I would accept the logical outcomes of my choices, now woven into this transformed horse-body: its hard sinews, its vulnerable flesh.

I went downstairs to the concierge, asked her to use her human fingers to make a phone call. Red-faced and excited, she rang Atalanta. They would send someone that afternoon, they said, to pick me up.

I did not call Serena. Maybe when I got down there. Perhaps, with all those miles between us, I wouldn't notice the bruise in her voice. By then, at any rate, I'd be easier to forgive: I would already be gone.

Q: Who are you?

A: Why does it matter?

Q: If I'm going to hand my whole life over, I don't want to give it to some faceless disembodied corporate entity, albeit one who quotes Spinoza. I want to know who's behind this whole thing.

A: But do you, really? If you could view the author(s) of these words as finite, defined by a particular gender and ethnicity and pattern of face and body hair, would you trust the process more? Or would you see your preju-

*dices reflected, or not reflected, and feel disappointed?
The word "corporate" is often used by liberals nowa-
days as a blanket put-down. With good reason: many
corporate entities in this country are rapacious and
amoral. But in this case we would like to remind you
where the word "corporate" comes from. It shares a root
with* corpus, body. *A corporate entity consists of many
bodies, aggregated into one; it then paradoxically becomes bodiless, capable of much more than any single
body might achieve. Our bodies themselves are corporate, made up of thousands upon thousands of
individual beings—not only cells and atoms, but other
living things, bacteria and other organisms too tiny for
the naked eye to record. Any body, in other words, is simultaneously a tightly arranged symphony and a
provisional, cacophonous jumble. Thus, any name I
could give myself would be no more than a useful lie, a
loosely hung banner, threadbare and flapping in the
wind.*

*Should you become a horse? I don't know. That's up
to you. However, keep in mind the above: if you transform into another sort of animal, it will only be a
steeper, more obvious transformation than the one you
would undergo anyway, as a human female becoming a
human female—always animal, always becoming.*

I have four horse-legs and a horse-torso and a horse-
head. Outwardly, at least, I am all animal.

I believe I still have a human brain, mostly—but every day, its language grows rougher around the edges. For minutes at a time, when I am running or eating in the pasture, I have no thoughts. My brain is not empty, exactly—it's as though a hot wind blows certain textures through my mind, shifts its responses to the world around it, to itself, in dark pleasurable ways that I cannot quite describe. My rage has diminished, but I am neither contained nor calm. I feel many emotions now, but they don't quite fit the words I know; I would describe them, mostly, as variations of active receptivity, of alert acceptance.

Somewhere, soon, Serena will be teaching her children the words for things. *This is a table. This is a chair. This is your mommy. This is a horse. This is the earth that ties you down, that holds you up.* Meanwhile my language is slowly departing, the words replaced by syllable and breath, *yes mm yes huh no hmmm brrrrrrrrr.* Long after I've lost my words completely, her kids will begin to ask her why: *why is the sky blue, why did I come out of your tummy, why don't we have a daddy or another mommy, why did Aunt Cassie become a horse?* She will struggle for answers; sometimes she will find them, and sometimes she won't. Sometimes she will sputter and snort, wave them away.

Maybe she'll come visit one day. Our final phone call, from the ranch, was brief, halting, awkward—but perhaps over time, in my absence, her hard judgments of me

AMY BONNAFFONS

О NS

will soften, turn into questions. They will lead her to me, across the long grass, and I'll look at her and nod. I'll recognize her. She won't try to ride me but I will allow her to approach, put a hand on my forehead, feel my horsey warmth.

There are touches like bridles you can kick away, and then there are touches that startle you into temporary submission, like the universe catching its breath: body against stunned body, mind against bright mind. A sudden snare of recognition. Wildness regarding itself.

BLACK STONES

To whom can we turn in our need? Not angels, not humans…

—Rilke

I.

At midnight, Sarah awoke to find an angel hovering above her hospital bed like a hummingbird. Aside from his large white wings, he looked like a regular naked man—but abnormally good-looking, with dark eyes and hunky shoulders. He wore a grave expression on his face.

"Oh," said Sarah. "I get it."

The angel shook his head. "Don't worry, you're not dead yet," he said. "This is just a preliminary visit."

He stilled his wings and floated downward, landing next to her, on his side. He folded his wings behind him and propped his head up on his elbow.

Sarah rolled onto her left side to face him. The rough blanket grated her skin, and she felt the ache in her abdomen where they'd cut her open. But then the angel reached out and touched her shoulder, and an amazing thing happened: all of the pain departed her body, in a great vertiginous rush so strong that she let out a little moan of pleasure.

"Open your mouth," he said. He slowly transferred a hard object from his tongue to hers. It felt smooth and round, like a stone. "Swallow it," he instructed, and she felt the little stone making its way down into the dark swamp of her insides.

He reached out and ran his warm callused hand down her side, and her body rose like bread. She could feel his straight and purposeful penis pressing into her leg. She started moving her hand in its direction.

But just then, as if this gesture reminded him of somewhere else he had to be, the angel leapt off the bed. He hovered above her again, beating his feathered wings.

"I'm going to come back tomorrow," he said. "I'm only authorized to give you one stone each day."

"I want you to stay," said Sarah. "I want to suck your cock."

"I know," he said. He glanced down with a slight shrug, as if to acknowledge, *who wouldn't?* "You can, eventually. And then, when you're ready, I'll perform intercourse with you, and you'll die. But everything has to happen in a certain order. That's what they told us, anyway."

"This is a stupid system," she said, bitterly.

He stared at her for a moment. "Maybe," he said. "But it's the only one there is. The only one I know of, anyway."

She closed her eyes, because it hurt to look at him. She kept them closed until her pain returned; when she opened them, he was gone.

II.

She couldn't hold even a smoothie down. She shook her head no.

Her husband, John, leaned back in the folding chair, the glass in his hand, the straw dangling off the side like an unanswered question.

"This is what I get for being a smart-ass," said Sarah. "When you don't take life seriously, death starts to take you seriously. It assumes you've been playing for the wrong team."

"Don't say that," said John.

"What, death?"

He closed his eyes. "Please stop."

"Maybe we could have a safe word," she said. "You

AMY BONNAFFONS

know, one of those phrases to prevent kinky sex from going too far. Like broccoli, or beeswax, or surfboard."

"Surfboard," he said.

He reached out and took her hand between his palms—the first time he'd touched her all day—and narrowed his gray eyes behind the black-framed glasses, as if trying to bring her more sharply into focus.

"Go home," she said. "I'll fall asleep in a minute, and then you should go home."

"I'm sorry."

"It's not your fault."

"No." He squeezed her hand tighter. "I mean—I'm *sorry*. For, you know—"

"Surfboard."

He cleared his throat. "I do love you, you know," he said. "Very much." She recognized the tone from his tort-law classes. *This is A Very Important Thing, what I'm saying.* Pompous and insincere. But she noticed that his hand, holding hers, was shaking.

She closed her eyes. She could have said something to ease his suffering, but she found that she didn't particularly care to.

She could still feel the angel's touch, humming inside her like brandy.

The angel returned just after midnight.

"Is it tomorrow already?" asked Sarah, turning to face him.

"Yeah." He leaned in and gave her another stone. She swallowed.

"Can I ask you something?"

"OK," he said.

"Is karma real?"

"I don't know what that is."

She frowned, and propped herself up on her elbow. "I'll tell you one thing," she said. "For all the sexy way they portray it in the movies, it's not very sexy to be the other woman. Because you're always the *other* woman. Never *the* woman, even if he ends up with you. At first John said he wanted kids with me. But now he comes back depressed from the custody visits with the kids he already has. It's terrible: he takes them out for lunch and they don't even talk to him, they just pull the batting out of rips in the diner seats while their ice cream melts."

"What's custody?"

"King Solomon. They cut the baby in half and nobody's happy."

"Whose baby?"

But she didn't answer.

"Now," she said, finally, "he's disgusted by my body. My skin feels like paper. I smell like sour milk." She lay back down, and pulled the blanket up around her shoulders. "He tries to hide it, but I can tell."

The angel stretched his wings, then folded them back again.

"I feel sad," he said, finally.

"Can you hold me?"

"Well—"

"I feel like it's the least you could do."

He got up and lay down next to her in the bed, climbing underneath the thin coverlet. He wrapped his arms around her.

"This is very uncomfortable for me," he confessed. "It just makes me want to have sex with you, and I can't do that. We're still in Prelims."

"I'm dying. My needs matter more than yours right now."

"I guess you're right." He pulled her a bit closer, and started to pat her lightly on the head. "Does this feel good?"

"Sort of."

He patted for a minute or two, and then he stopped, resting his arm down the length of her side.

"I want to say the nicest possible thing to you," he said.

"Tell me I'm beautiful," she whispered.

"You're beautiful. I really want to have sex with you right now, because you're so beautiful. But I can't."

She still said nothing, but her rib cage rose and fell more rapidly.

"Do you want me to tell you anything else?" he offered.

"No, thanks," she said. "That was fine." But her voice was small and tight and distant.

A thin strip of lemon light showed beneath the industrial-gray hospital blinds. This meant the angel was already late for his next client—high school girl, car accident. After that he was supposed to visit a housewife counting the pills in her cabinet, contemplating suicide.

The black stones lay tucked in the folds of his wings, waiting. But he couldn't bring himself to leave.

THE CLEAS

I found the Cleas on Craigslist, accidentally, while looking for a mattress frame. The ad said *Two families looking to share after-school care for six-year-old girls. You: energetic young woman who loves kids. Background in art/early childhood education/creative movement a plus!!!* I didn't know about any of those things, but I needed money. Applying for graduate school was more expensive than I'd realized, and revising my undergraduate thesis on the complexity of Beyoncé as a feminist icon was taking longer than I'd thought. I'd begun stealing tampons and energy bars from my dog-walking clients. *Extensive experience with young children,* I wrote in my email. *Whiz at arts and crafts!*

They didn't call my bluff, or my references. At my interview, I learned that the moms had met at a Gotham Kidz Club and become friends upon discovering that their daughters had the same name. They were both named Clea. (One was short for Cleopatra, and the other was not short for anything.) Then they discovered other similarities: they lived three blocks away from each other on Riverside Drive; the four parents, between them, had five Ph.D.s.

When I met the girls, I could not believe they were the same age. One Clea had about thirty pounds on the other. The bigger Clea was a stocky blond peasant type with a big gap between her front teeth. The smaller Clea looked vaguely malnourished, with large eyes in a pale heart-shaped face. They told me I could call them Big Clea and Small Clea. I said I would not do that, it was horrible to define someone by their body.

"I don't mind," said Small Clea.

"I do," I said. "Pick a new name."

Big Clea thought for a minute. "I choose Rainbow Clea," she said.

Small Clea just stared at me and stuck her pointer finger up her nose.

"Don't you want a pretty new name?" I said.

"I don't care," she said, and shrugged. Then she said, "OK. I choose Grass Clea."

I thought this choice was unfortunate, but I did not force her to change it because it was her life, not mine.

Then Rainbow Clea turned to Grass Clea and said, "Let's play Slave."

"OK," said Grass Clea. She lay down on the floor and Rainbow Clea began to whip her with a fun noodle.

I wondered how they knew about slaves. Or why they had a fun noodle—there wasn't a pool or anything. I thought, isn't it interesting how quickly children's relational personalities solidify into dominant and submissive. I considered the early-childhood roots of violence. I'd come up with several plausible theories for Rainbow Clea's behavior before I realized it was my job to stop it.

I picked the Cleas up from school on the Upper East Side every afternoon, waiting along with the blond mothers in Banana Republic or Lululemon and the Caribbean nannies in long skirts. I was the one thing not like the others. I wore dime-store earrings, duct-taped boots, hoodies, and leggings stretched from too many wearings between Laundromat trips: the uniform of the white twentysomething with a liberal arts degree and Medicaid, perpetually on the verge of a graduate program.

We'd go to this one playground in Central Park that had several knee-high hippopotamus statues, and the Cleas would pretend to ride them. Sometimes I squatted down onto a hippopotamus myself, and they shrieked with pleasure. There was probably something Freudian about their reaction, but I did not pursue the line of thought.

Sometimes, I just sat on a bench and watched them from the corner of my eye while texting the person I was sleeping with. At the moment, this was Zander, who I'd met at a midnight screening of *Rear Window*, because we

AMY BONNAFFONS

were the only people there. I was there because I'd been bored in my apartment, and he was there because he was homeless. So I took him home, which worked out well for both of us: he had a place to sleep, and I was no longer bored. In fact, I learned something important that night about Zander: he had a zeal for cunnilingus, a real one, not one he affected to seem like a feminist. Some guys think you can't tell, but you can.

He also had one habit I did not like, which was touching my face all over with his fingertips in between make-out sessions, like a blind guy in the movies. Some people find this romantic. I find it creepy. But I did not stop him.

In case you were wondering, Zander wasn't homeless as in sleeping on the street. He was homeless as in he'd forgotten to re-sign his lease, so his landlord had evicted him and he was temporarily couch-surfing, which sounds like more fun than it actually is.

The morning after—which was very morning-aftery, bleary and incandescent—I went to my dog-walking job, and left Zander my keys so he could sleep late. That afternoon, he met me in Central Park to drop them off.

I was playing with Rainbow and Grass on the hippopotamus playground. When he called out my name, I acted shocked to see him. "What a surprise!" I said. (This was the agreed-upon signal, to make our meeting appear accidental.)

Zander spoke his line: "Tess! Hi! I was just walking by, and I saw you."

"Girls," I said, "this is my friend Zander."

"Nice to meet you ladies," said Zander, and he grinned.

Let me describe Zander. He was like a sexy clown. He played accordion in a band called Baby. They were big in the Bushwick scene. He wore an old tweed jacket with elbow patches that was about two sizes too big. He had a lean body and a lopsided smile and a face as pretty as a girl's: dark curly hair and eyelashes long and black like calligraphy brushes. Most noticeably, though, he had extremely unusual eyes.

"Your eyes are two different colors," observed Rainbow Clea.

"Yeah," chimed Grass. "One green and one blue."

"That's true," said Zander, thoughtfully, as if he'd never considered this fact before. "You know, it must be because my mom is part mermaid."

The Cleas' eyes widened like satellite dishes.

"Like Ariel?" whispered Grass Clea.

"Yeah," he said. "But she has legs and stuff. She's only part." He shrugged self-effacingly.

Rainbow Clea was about to lose her shit. She actually started hopping from one leg to another. "Rainbow, do you have to go to the bathroom?" I asked.

She didn't hear me. She was about to explode with the effort of racking her brain for the thing that would most impress Zander.

"I have a guinea pig!" she finally yelled.

"It actually belongs to our class?" said Grass. "Its name is Toothbrush, and—"

"We voted about what to name it," interrupted Rainbow.

" 'Toothbrush' was my idea," said Grass.

Rainbow stood stricken mute; she had no idea how to compete with this.

"Did you guys know that guinea pigs aren't actually pigs?" said Zander.

"Yeah, obviously," said Rainbow, thrilled and grateful at the change of subject.

"Yeah, obviously," echoed Grass.

"They're related to trolls," said Zander.

Rainbow frowned. "That's not true," she said.

"You think so?" said Zander. "Well, the next time you see a troll, look closer."

They stared up at him. They were two girls in love. Collectively, we were two girls in love and one girl who'd achieved an almost poetic level of horniness.

"Come away with me to the hippos, Zander," said Rainbow, breathlessly, like she was asking him to elope. She grabbed his hand.

"Okay, for a minute," he said. But as the girls turned and ran in the direction of the statues, he slipped his hand into my back pocket and cupped his palm against my butt. Then he slid it back out, leaving my keys. I had to give it to him: that was a nice touch.

Over the next few weeks, I texted Zander the funny

things that Grass and Rainbow did. He texted back lots of emoticons, and asked to see me.

We hardly ever met up, though; I usually lied and said I was busy. When I like someone, I try to keep things hypothetical for as long as possible. Everything eventually disappoints. There's always that moment of turning away, on one side or the other. The best part is the waiting: you're Ariel on the rock, windblown, full of desire.

During these weeks, Grass Clea developed a new and eccentric clothing habit. She insisted on wearing the same outfit every day: black leggings, black Mary Janes, and a brown cable-knit sweater of her mother's that she'd retrieved from the dirty-clothes hamper. The sweater reached down to her ankles, the sleeves dangling limply several inches below her hands. It was cute, in a disturbing sort of way. She looked like a little Precious Moments street urchin. She called the sweater Mommy's Dirty Sweater, and then just the Dirty—"Dirty" apparently both modifying the noun and serving as a noun itself. Once a week, her mother managed to wrestle her out of the Dirty long enough to wash it. But during the wash cycle Clea grew extremely anxious. She'd press her face to the washing machine, weeping quietly. Her mother would try to tempt her away—with Dora the Explorer, with Barbie, with Popsicles—but she wouldn't budge. The cleaning process was a kind of death, one for which she was never prepared. She mourned the sweater's absence like a military wife; she moaned and twisted her hair, refusing comfort. When it eventually came out of the dryer, she put it on and hugged herself into a tight, fetal little ball and whispered unintelligible messages into her stomach.

I wondered if she was depressed. I wondered if it was possible to be depressed at six. Then I thought, if anyone could, it would be Grass Clea.

Let me describe Grass Clea's family. Her two parents had three Ph.D.s: in Russian Literature, German Moral Philosophy, and Holocaust Studies. The mother, Nadine, had the same wispy hair and large eyes—the same starving-alien beauty—as her daughter. When we got home, we usually found her sitting in an armchair with a book in her lap, staring into space, frowning. (She was the one with the Russian and Holocaust degrees.) Walter, the dad, was a little uptight, but at least he tried to have fun. He had one joke. His joke was the German language. He put "das" in front of everything. Like "das macaroni" or "das pajamas." Nadine did not find this joke funny. Neither did Clea, really, but she smiled weakly anyway.

Ann, the mother of Rainbow Clea, was different. She had a high blond ponytail and did yoga every day and kept a piece of paper taped to the refrigerator that said "Keep the channel open!—Martha Graham." I wondered if she thought about Martha Graham every time she opened the freezer for a SoyPop. I wondered if it made her happy or sad. I wondered if, in her estimation, her own channel was open. Her daughter's certainly was. Once when I stayed for dinner, Rainbow Clea said, "You know, Miss Heidi should really wax her armpits," and Ann hooted with delight. (Miss Heidi, the Cleas' teacher, was the kind of hairy, organic, unapologetic feminist who always made me feel vaguely threatened and inadequate, though in theory I supported her choices.)

Like Walter, Ann had one joke. Her joke was sticking her hand in a sock to create a puppet that spoke in an accent somewhere between Russian and French. It said, "I vill poot it in zee microwave!" or "No Popseecle vissout zee vegetables!"

Ann referred to female genitalia as "the peeps," which Clea explained was short for "peepeemaker." This euphemism bothered me—so incomplete!—but I chose not to interfere. She encouraged Clea to sleep without underwear; at night the puppet said, "Don't forget to air out zee peeps!"

I was already three or four weeks into the job when I met Ann's husband, David. Rainbow Clea and I came in from the playground one day and found him in the kitchen.

"Hi, Daddy!" yelled Clea.

"Hi, princess," he said. But he was looking at me. He was absurdly handsome, like a cartoon superhero, with black hair and a cleft chin.

"So," he said. "You're the famous Tess. The Cleas' new

AMY BONNAFFONS

favorite person. Let me see. From Illinois or one of the other *I* states? Creative Movement at Bennington?"

"Iowa. And Body and Media Studies."

"Ah, I see. What did that involve? A lot of interpretive dance to Jodorowsky films?" He smirked, in a way that was somehow both derisive and intimate, as if we were in on the same joke, the joke that was me.

I frowned. "Well," I said, "it was mostly analysis of pop culture. My thesis—"

"Daddy!" yelled Clea. "Want to play Candyland?"

David glanced toward his daughter. "We'll both play"—he opened the refrigerator, keeping his eyes on me—"if Tess will let me get her a glass of wine." He pulled out a bottle of white. "Don't worry. You're officially off-duty."

He didn't give me a chance to say no—just expertly extracted the cork, *pop,* and poured a glass with a deft flick of the wrist. Then he handed it to me, again with that smirk. This time, I understood, the smirk referred to both of us, to the scene we were playing out: the sexy husband handing a glass of wine to the nubile messy-haired babysitter. Wasn't it funny that we were enacting these tropes? Wasn't it clever and postmodern of us to mock them through inhabiting them, to ironically reappropriate this clichéd moment? Wouldn't I join him in the joke?

I shrugged and accepted the glass of wine, although I had already decided, officially, that I disapproved of David Wright. He was just an older version of the hipster boys I'd messed with in college, whose every action exuded a whiff of mockery—for whom even the human body was such a cliché that they could barely bring themselves to have sex unironically. They'd rub their bony hips against yours in a way that seemed more expressive of annoyance than desire; then they'd ejaculate perfunctorily and offer you a cigarette. You'd walk-of-shame home clutching your jacket around you, embarrassed by the obviousness of your breasts, the slime in your underpants.

So I was somewhat surprised to see David Wright, playing Candyland, become distinctly silly. He had a different voice for each of the characters, and unlike his wife, he displayed an effortless mastery of accent and dialect. The witch in the Peanut Brittle House sounded like a Yiddish washerwoman; the smiling lollipops were garrulous Venezuelans; the Gingerbread Man spoke in a nasal, hesitation-riddled voice that reminded me of Steve Buscemi. When Clea advanced up the Gumdrop Trail, skipping several spaces ahead of him, David let out a comic howl of consternation, provoking a cascade of giggles. When I then drew the Lollipop Card and left them both in the dust, he distracted her by making up a song that went "Revenge! Revenge! Revenge shall be mine!" and chanting it along with her until she'd overtaken me again. Clea spent the whole game either delirious with laughter or reverently looking up at her father, waiting for his next move, practically vibrating with adoration.

Was he a good dad, or an attention-loving narcissist? Was there a faint air of mockery, or self-mockery, to even his performance of fatherhood? Either way, I'd fallen a little bit in love with him, in spite of myself, by the time Ann walked in, clearly fresh from yoga: blond wisps escaping her loose ponytail, cheeks flushed, spandexed body high and firm. "Hello, my leetle petoonia!" she called to Clea. "Hi, Tess."

She didn't say hello to her husband. She didn't need to. In the dark looks they shot each other, I perceived their whole relationship, which is to say I understood their sex: Ann's cheesiness transmuted into kooky, panting energy, David's coldness shaming her into even deeper excitement. I could see the venom with which they'd attack each other, as soon as their daughter was safely stowed away in her big-girl bed.

I politely excused myself. As soon as I was out of the building, I called Zander and told him to come over. Something restless had gotten into me, and my waiting felt lonely. I felt like my body was heating up, its molecules moving in greater and greater arcs; if I did not act soon, I might become a liquid or gas.

"I want you to lie on top of me," I said. "I want you to be as heavy as possible."

"I want to do more than lie on top of you," he said, kissing my neck.

"Whatever," I said. "Just stop wasting time."

We collapsed onto the couch and for a brief and delicious period of time, he did exactly what I wanted, which was to cover my whole body with his mouth. But then he did what I'd feared: he murmured a quiet question, to which I nodded with resignation, and then he put on a condom and began to fuck me very gently.

"Harder," I told him. "Harder." He obeyed, but it didn't help. He'd opened the wrong door, and I'd flown away, and I couldn't get myself back.

In theory I do not approve of faking, but in practice it's easier than explaining. I prefer to call it performing, and over time I've grown expert: the breathing that quickens to match my partner's, the soft moans, the desperate yelps that signal the formal end of another person's responsibility for my pleasure.

When I sensed that Zander was close, I panted, yelped, allowed my breaths to slow—all from a great distance, as if by remote control. When he slumped onto my chest, spent from the hot bright journey he'd made alone, I slid out from beneath him.

The countdown had begun. I could see how the rest of this would play out. We'd sleep together a few more times, he'd say some tender gooshy things, and then he'd brush up against this cold part of me that repels other people the way the wrong end of a magnet does, and he'd start to drift away from me, and I'd let him.

And where did this big cold magnet thing come from? When did I absorb this allergy to the gentle fuck, this contempt for tenderness? Anyhow, at least the flying-away feeling was gone.

The next day, when I went to pick the Cleas up from school, Miss Heidi of the second-wave armpits pulled me aside. The girls were playing one of those games that involves hand slapping and a singsongy chant with dark psychological undertones. *Miss Lucy had a baby, she named him Tiny Tim, she put him in the bathtub to see if he could swim.*

"Clea Stein"—that's Grass Clea—"had a little, ah, incident today," said Miss Heidi. "I've already called her mother. She"—Miss Heidi glanced over at the two girls—"well, she bit another student."

"Don't all kids go through a biting phase?"

"Not usually when they're six. And when I asked her why she bit Evelyn, she said, because Evelyn was being a"—here Miss Heidi leaned in and whispered an unspeakable word—*the* unspeakable word—into my ear.

I pulled back. "She *said* that?"

Miss Heidi nodded. "Afraid so."

I took the two Cleas' hands as we left the school. "Am I going to get in trouble?" asked Grass Clea, hopefully. I frowned.

"Obviously," said Rainbow Clea.

"I don't know," I said. "It's up to your mommy."

"My mommy won't care."

"I'm sure you had a good reason to be angry," I said.

"I wasn't *angry*," said Grass. "It was part of the game."

"What game?"

She shrugged. "The *game*."

I paused. "Did Evelyn know that it was part of the game?"

She shrugged again. I let it go.

That night, when we got to Grass's house, we found Nadine hovering in the kitchen, rather than sitting in her habitual staring-chair by the window. She exchanged a serious look with me, then crouched down so that her face was level with her daughter's.

"You're not to say that word ever again," she said.

"What word?" said Clea.

"The word you said to Evelyn today. Do you even know what it means?"

"It means...like, stupid."

"No, it doesn't," said Nadine. She stood up and paced back and forth across the kitchen. "It doesn't mean that." She crouched down again. "Who did you hear it from?"

"I don't know."

"From kids in your class? Clea Wright?" She lowered her voice, confidentially. "Or her parents?"

Clea shrugged. Nadine was standing now, arms folded, looking down at her daughter with a weary expression, as if she'd known all along that this day might come.

The next day, Ann picked up Rainbow Clea from school herself, unconvincingly claiming a forgotten doctor's visit. She greeted me, and Miss Heidi, as exuberantly as ever, but didn't acknowledge Grass Clea's presence; she seemed to carefully avoid even looking in the child's direction. Did Rainbow's sudden "appointment" have something to do with the other Clea's utterance of the Unspeakable Word? Was it possible, for Ann, that one's channel could become *too* open?

Grass Clea and I had never spent the afternoon without Rainbow. I'd always favored her in my heart, but being alone with her was surprisingly awkward. I hadn't realized how much Rainbow Clea contributed to the dynamic, how much my relationship with Grass depended on triangulation.

On the way home, I tried initiating a heart-to-heart. "You know," I said, "about your sweater? When I was younger I had a favorite outfit too. I had this Cinderella nightgown, which used to belong to my older sister Grace, who I thought was the coolest person ever. So I didn't want to let go of it, even when my mom told me I'd gotten too big."

Grass Clea looked thoughtful for a moment, like I'd really gotten through to her. "You know," she said, "cockroaches are smaller than mice. But they run faster."

I gave up. Who could tell the reason behind the sweater, behind anything?

"When you were a kid," I asked Zander that night, "do you think you were, like, aware of your parents' happiness or unhappiness?" We had just shared a pizza on my couch. We were leaning against each other, and his hand was on my thigh and starting to slowly crawl upward, but I wasn't really in the mood yet.

"What do you mean?" He stilled his fingers for a moment.

"Like, do you think their mood affected yours."

"Of course it did. How could it not?"

"Yeah."

"Like, when my parents got divorced, my dad was like that character in *Peanuts* with the constant cloud of dirt around him. But with sadness. For years."

I pictured Zander, for a moment, as a child; he must have been heartbreakingly adorable, with those long lashes and weird beautiful eyes. Surging with a sudden tenderness for him, for the boy inside the man, I leaned over and kissed him deeply, playing my fingers over the edges of his ears. He responded hungrily, pulling my hips onto his and running his fingers through my hair as we kissed. But after a minute or two, he pulled away.

"What about you?"

"What about me what?"

"Were your parents unhappy?"

That was the kind of guy he was: the kind who cared about conversational parity, who would even pause sex in order to ensure it.

Instead of answering, I leaned in and kissed him, harder than I had before. I ground my hips against his.

He moaned and pulled me in closer and told me I was beautiful and I felt a little twinge of gratitude and tenderness and said "You too."

But when he gently made his way inside of me it was David Wright's face that abruptly appeared in my mind, smirking at me, as if he knew my secret: my disdain for the trap of this body; my yearning to explode it from the inside; my fear that, after such an explosion, there would be nothing of me left.

In order to avoid this image, and what it implied, I opted to exit my body. I hovered several inches above the couch. First I focused on Zander. I watched him having sex with me. I felt mildly envious; he seemed like he was having a really good time. Then I focused on myself. I thought about how my face and body must look, in ostensible erotic transport—the *o* of my mouth, the flush of my cheeks, the muss of my hair. The image pleased me. I exaggerated my facial expression, and a moan escaped my mouth. This was my most reliable route to sexual pleasure: it was like I was fucking myself, through Zander, and thus having sex while simultaneously avoiding it.

"I feel like you're not really here," he said, afterward. We'd just finished, and he was holding me, doing the blind-guy thing to my face. "Are you OK?"

Briefly, I considered trying to actually answer his question. Then Grass popped into my mind, big-eyed in her dirty brown sweater. And I thought: where would I start.

The obvious tension between the families continued for about a week; Rainbow Clea rejoined us, but I perceived a sudden distance between the two girls. I wondered how much longer our arrangement would last.

Then, one rainy Friday, I was given money to take the Cleas to a movie. Unfortunately for me, they decided on a B-grade Pixar rip-off with environmental themes: a buxom, green-skinned fairy named Chloroplastia battles with evil condo developers to save the organic bean farm on which she and her fairy rock band record hits like "My Seed Is Your Seed" and "Worms!"

The movie made me want to stick razors in my eyes, but it seemed to restore the Cleas' relationship: they exited the theater holding hands, and on the crosstown bus home they made me Google the lyrics to "Worms!"

"Let me ask you a question," I said, as we approached Columbus. "Why do you think Chloroplastia fell in love with Bio D-Grade the Composting Rapper?"

"Because there was a spell on her, obviously," said Rainbow Clea.

"I think it's because he sang good," said Grass Clea.

"That's incorrect," I said. "It's because the movies want to make you believe that you can't do anything unless you're somebody's girlfriend. It's not true."

"Are you Zander's girlfriend?" asked Grass Clea.

"That is personal information," I said.

"My dad has a girlfriend," said Rainbow.

"What?"

"He does," she said. "I saw them once. In the park. I was on the bus. They were standing next to a bench and he was petting her butt."

I was speechless. I couldn't say David's unfaithfulness came as a huge surprise, but this public display of butt-petting? Rainbow's best quality was her oneness with her id, and yet this distorted primal scene seemed enough to permanently disfigure anyone.

"I didn't see the lady," said Rainbow. "Just her back. She was really small and she was wearing a hat."

"How did you feel?"

Rainbow shrugged. "She wasn't naked, so it's OK."

I couldn't bring myself to explain the flaw in this logic. "How about you guys sing 'Worms!' again?"

"Yeah!" they cried, and David's girlfriend was forgotten, at least for the moment.

Worms! They are nature's recyclers
Worms! They make our plants fertiliiiiized
Worms! They are vegetable-likers
Worms! What a slimy surprise!

I dropped Rainbow off first, leaving her with the housekeeper. When we arrived at Grass's door, it swung open before I could knock, to reveal a haggard-looking Nadine.

"There you are!" she cried. She looked even paler than usual, her face tear-streaked and raw, dark hair matted strangely to one side of her head. "I left you like five messages. I just got a call from Connecticut. My mother's in the hospital."

"Oh my God. I'm sorry. What's wrong?"

"They're not sure. They think a stroke. She's still unconscious."

"Jesus. Sorry, the girls were playing with my phone. What can I do?"

"I know it's extremely short notice," she said, "but can you stay over tonight? Walter's at that Kant conference in Seattle." She hugged herself, like she was cold: a little girl without her mother. "I just need to get out there ASAP."

"Of course."

"Is Oma going to be OK?" asked Clea.

Nadine looked down at her in surprise, like she'd forgotten she was somebody's mother as well as somebody's daughter. "I don't know," she said. She reached down and mussed Clea's hair, then wandered off to her bedroom to pack.

When Nadine had gone, I ordered a pizza and told Clea she could stay up late. Then I rigged an endless DVR loop of Dora the Explorer, hoping Dora's unrelenting positivity and vigor would have some kind of reassuring effect.

I sat very close to Clea on the giant lumpen couch, so that she could snuggle if she felt like it. It seemed like snuggling ought to be something I should offer at a time like this. But I wouldn't initiate. I found myself infected by an exaggerated respect for her boundaries. She was more private than most adults; she wouldn't take well to the condescension of an unsolicited cuddle. So we sat there mutely watching the antics of Map and Backpack, until she suddenly stood up.

"I'm tired," she announced.

"Do you want to go to bed?"

"Yes."

"Okay. Let's get you into pajamas."

She shook her head. "I want to sleep in the Dirty."

I hesitated; was it my job to cajole her into something more appropriate? Or should I let her get comfort where she could? "Okay," I relented. "But just for tonight."

Clea brushed her teeth and used the bathroom. Then she got under the covers.

"You can leave now," she said.

"You don't want me to stay?"

She didn't answer for such a long time that I thought she wasn't going to. Then, in a small voice, she said: "Yes. Stay."

"All right," I said, relieved; I'd felt a terrible foreboding against leaving her alone. I sat in the chair next to her bed for a while, but it was impossible to tell when she'd really fallen asleep. Finally I stood up and tiptoed over to the bed. I observed her unmoving doll-like face, her shallow breathing. She had to be asleep, right? Yet there was something about her, a tension that her little body held even in repose, that made me doubt myself. It was possible that she was a superb faker; it was also possible that, even in sleep, she remained alert. "Good night, Clea," I whispered. When she didn't respond, I left the room.

Back in the kitchen, I opened the refrigerator to snoop. I hoped to come across some expensive tapenade or cheese, or at least some Häagen-Dazs. That was the best part of babysitting: you got to eat all their stuff when the kid fell asleep.

But Nadine and Walter's refrigerator was like a vision of some terrible past or future. The top shelf was occupied by six Tupperwares, into which celery sticks were packed like cigarettes. You could tell from the sheer volume that not just one but all three members of this family regularly ate a Tupperware of celery for lunch. The only other items were a tub of plain yogurt, half a gallon of skim milk, and a jar of beet borscht. I felt suddenly crippled by sadness.

I took my phone out of my pocket and texted Zander: *spending the night at nadine and walter's. want to pay me a bad-girl visit on the upper west?*

His response came immediately: *be there by midnight.*

While I waited for him, I watched a game show called *Secret Secrets Are No Fun*, an updated version of *The Newlywed Game.* The first question was "What's the craziest place you've ever had sex?" Jake and Jessika, from Atlanta, both said "On an airplane" and passed Round 1. Harold and Arlene, retirees from Wisconsin, fared less well. Arlene said "My sister's house" and Harold said "Standing up." Just as the Deduction Buzzer rang, I heard a key turning in the lock.

I looked up, confused: it was too early for Zander. But, just as it occurred to me that he didn't have a key anyway, I watched the door swing open to reveal David Wright. We regarded each other across the room with a pulse of disbelief.

I stood up. "Nadine's mother is in the hospital," I said. "She went to Connecticut. I'm staying over."

He remained in the doorway, one hand on the knob. "Ah," he said. "I see. So I guess she was distracted. I was supposed to—"

He stopped short of offering an explanation, because we each suddenly knew that the other knew why David was really there. A quick montage flashed through my mind: the small hatted girlfriend, the subterranean distrust between the two families. Of course: the tension was about more than a child's utterance of a forbidden word.

But how deep did it go? Were David and Nadine conducting a juicy, old-fashioned affair, or was there some kind of complex sexual arrangement between the two families, one that required the maintenance of a delicate emotional balance, upset by the smallest transgression? Just because I'd rifled through their kitchens, played with their children, I imagined I'd *known* these people—but I could hardly surmise the precise contours, the byzantine rules, of their adult games. I was basically a child myself.

David and I stared at each other, saying nothing. Slowly that mocking smile crept into his face. He was coming to find the situation amusing.

He hung his jacket on a hook by the door, casually, as if he lived here (which maybe, it occurred to me, he kind of did); he advanced toward me across the kitchen, that smile growing deeper and more knowing as he drew closer; he paused and turned toward a cabinet, then extracted a bottle of red wine from the back.

Whatever he was going to do or not do, he was going to make me wait for it. He poured two glasses and handed me one, just as he had at his apartment that day. Our eyes met over the rims of our wide wineglasses, but still neither of us said anything. I could tell he was relishing the moment, its saturation with erotic cliché. I, on the other hand, was unable to feel any sort of irony. I was deeply, terrifyingly in my body; my heart pounded in fear, and I was soaking wet.

"My boyfriend is coming over," I blurted. "In about an hour."

"Ah," said David. This seemed to amuse him even more deeply. "I see."

"Well, he's not really my boyfriend, exactly."

"Hm. Interesting." He took a sip of wine. "And this nonboyfriend is named?"

"Zander."

"Zander. That sounds about right. Let me guess, he's a deejay? Or maybe he plays the drums? The accordion?"

I blushed so hard I didn't need to answer. David laughed.

That was when it became unbearable for me: not my desire but my nerves, my terror of this moment, my embarrassment at the obviousness of my discomfort. I reached out and seized the moment by its belt buckle. I planted a kiss on the moment's rough, derisive mouth.

David made a noise that was simultaneously a laugh and a murmur of pleasure; then he reached down and lifted me up onto the kitchen island and deftly pinned both my wrists behind me with one arm. He slid his other hand up my skirt and whispered, "See how wet you are. I knew it. I knew you were a hungry little cunt." Then he shoved two fingers inside me, hard, and I gasped with shock and pleasure.

He had succeeded: he had caught me off guard. For a few minutes he touched me in a way that was so rough and delicious that I didn't care at all about the fact that I didn't like or approve of him, didn't care that Zander was coming, didn't even care about the fact that there was a small child in the next room, that this encounter would surely cost me my job; I just wanted him inside of me. I wanted, for once, to be fucked correctly, in a way that acknowledged and made use of my darkness.

But David Wright did not fuck me. Just at the moment when he should have—just at the moment when it became imperative for him to fuck me—he withdrew his hand and slid it down into his own pants.

He worked with grim purpose, with total control. I was too stunned to say anything. Soon he let out a curt, strangled cry and came onto my skirt, in a dark splotch just above my right hip. Only then did his other hand let go of my wrists.

It was the most specific and expert way I'd ever been disrespected. As he zipped himself up, I opened my mouth, about to voice some kind of protest—but then he looked up with a grin, and I realized I had it all wrong.

He thought I'd *liked* it, what he'd just done. Was this what he did with Nadine, with his wife? Had other women pretended to enjoy watching him masturbate? He kept smiling at me as he buckled his belt, in a way that conveyed his sense that things had gone exactly as they should have.

In theory, my feminist education had prepared me well for a moment such as this. Sitting around the seminar table, I could have come up with an articulate rebuttal to David Wright's unspoken assumptions. But now there was the fact of him standing above me, wearing that grin; there was the fact of his splooge on my skirt, and of the cold granite of Nadine and Walter's countertop beneath my ass, and I found I had no words.

He reached out and cupped my cheek in his hand. "You're so young," he said. He smiled with a serene self-satisfaction so radiant, it almost resembled tenderness. "So lovely and young."

After David left, I took off my skirt in the bathroom and, hands shaking, tried to wash the stain out of it. Of course, I just succeeded in getting the entire skirt wet. So I hung it over the shower-curtain rod to dry. At least I was still wearing leggings beneath.

Then, with a rush of guilt, I remembered Clea.

I tiptoed over to her door and gently eased it open. She lay there on her back, in the same position I'd left her, but with her eyes wide open, staring up at the ceiling.

She must have heard everything. What kinds of adult darkness had her little body registered, seismographically, while she lay there in that narrow bed? How many times had she overheard this "game"—David Wright messing with her mother, using the unspeakable word she'd learned to repeat? Did she now assume that being messed with by David Wright was a rite of passage for all adult women? If she had somehow been able to articulate this in the form of a question—if she'd been able to ask me which rites of passage were unavoidable, and which were disgusting and which desirable, and how to navigate them—what could I tell her? What did I even know?

"Clea," I said.

She didn't respond. The long limp sleeves of the Dirty lay on top of the covers, empty; for some reason, this image flooded me with despair.

"Clea," I said.

"What?"

"Why are you awake?"

"I don't know."

"Maybe you should put on some pajamas. What if you took off the Dirty and put on some pajamas?"

"No."

"Please?"

"No."

My phone beep-beeped in my pocket: probably Zander, texting to announce his presence in the lobby. I ignored it.

"Your phone," said Clea. "It beeped."

"I know," I said. "I heard it."

"When the phone rings," said Clea, "you have to answer. Otherwise something bad happens."

"Who told you that?"

"No one," she said. "I just know things."

I picked up the phone and looked at it. *Here!* it said. *How do I get in?*

I left Clea, closing the door behind me, and approached the complicated buzzer by the front door: a gray box with a speaker and three unmarked buttons. Which button did I press to allow him into the building? Was he supposed to press first, or did he have to wait on me? Why were there no instructions? I suddenly felt very tired, so tired I could cry.

I have to figure out how this stupid buzzer thing works, I texted.

I'm not going anywhere, he said.

I pressed all three buttons simultaneously—fuck it—then pressed them again, hoping at least one of them would do the trick: would send the correct message down into the building's nervous system, move its muscles and bones, cause it to open itself up and allow this stranger inside.

A ROOM
TO LIVE IN

> Beauty is a matter of size and order, and
> therefore impossible either (1) in a very
> minute creature as it approaches instan-
> taneity; or (2) in a creature of vast size—
> one, say, 1,000 miles long.
>
> —Aristotle

I decided to give the boys little slingshots and toy trains.
For the girl, I made a tiny doll; I had to use my most powerful magnifying glass to paint the freckles and eyelashes.

"Classic, well appointed," Mrs. Perlman had told me
over the phone. "Deep plush carpets, a piano, filigreed
wallpaper in the master bedroom." She hoped for me to
re-create, in miniature, the apartment in Vienna where
her mother had lived as a child, before the war sent the

family into poverty and exile. There were two boys and one girl, though one of the boys—Otto—had died in transit.

I gave him the better slingshot.

Carl and I were washing the dishes that night, in our usual way (side by side, I in rubber gloves, he armed with a towel), when he abruptly cleared his throat. "I was thinking," he said, carefully, "that we could do something."

"You mean sex?"

"Well, actually, I was thinking in larger terms."

"What terms?"

"Well, I was thinking we could have a child."

"Tonight?"

"No, just sometime."

"I don't know. Where would it sleep?"

"Well, it could sleep in my room, and I could sleep in yours."

"Where would I sleep?"

"In your room too."

"With you?"

"Yes."

We'd been over this before. Carl had suggested, many times, that as my husband he had the right to share my bed. But I always maintained that anything seen too close up grows fuzzy and indistinct. Carl's head next to mine on the pillow displaced too much air, the wrong air.

I could only see one of his features at a time: his nose, or his eyelashes, or his nipple. It gave me a sort of horizontal vertigo.

But sometimes, when I peered through his open doorway and saw him sitting on the floor cross-legged, plucking his banjo, I felt a desire of exactly the right size. Then, when the desire grew bigger, I asked my feet to take me into his room. They obliged. Then our bodies asked things of each other, and they obliged too.

"Carl," I said. "You know how I feel about that."

"Well, I know the words you've told me before," he said.

"I'll try to think of other ones."

"This isn't an issue of words, really, though. It's more an issue of our bodies and where we put them."

"I suppose so," I said. "I'll think about it."

Later, in my own room, I thought about it. I tried to think with my body and not just with words. I tried to trick my body into different positions, to put a new angle on things. I lay prone on my bed, then sat on the floor with legs splayed wide, then attempted a headstand against the wall and failed. My body made a loud noise when it crashed to the floor.

"You OK?" Carl called.

"Yes," I called back. But I was curled in a fetal position, clutching my knees to my chest. This seemed to be the default position I ended up in when I thought about

Changing Things. I did this only when Carl asked me to: infrequently in the first few months of our marriage, and then more and more often, and then pretty much weekly. Tonight marked an escalation in the seriousness of the request; Carl's dissatisfaction with our system had grown more urgent. When I thought of his unhappiness growing sharper and sharper, like some pointed thing, I grew unhappy too.

But I still couldn't imagine sharing my bed every night, let alone having a third person in the apartment, someone possibly very loud, who oozed bodily fluid and need. No, no, my position wouldn't change.

I used my hands to pry my knees away from my body. I got up and did the only thing that reliably calmed me: I got to work.

I carved the two younger children from imported Tahitian balsa wood, with a blade designed to perform thoracic surgery on insects. I modeled them after a blurry black-and-white photograph Mrs. Perlman had provided. In the photo, the family stood squinting in the bright sun. The parents, in back, were the kind of couple who looked like siblings (parallel genetics? or a harsh molding by convergent life experience?)—both thin and pinched-looking, with the same severe shoulders and eyebrows.

The sun shone down on the children, twelve-year-old Franz and eight-year-old twins Otto and Gretel. Franz had curly hair and the open, handsome face of a future homecoming king. (He killed himself in 1972.) Gretel had two braids wound tightly around her ears, like Princess Leia. She had fat cheeks and an impish smile, a girl who clearly expected to be fed and loved ceaselessly. (She grew up to be the mother of Mrs. Perlman and of two other children who both died in infancy. She lives in a nursing home in Bedford, New York.)

Otto, on the other hand, was thin and angular, like his parents, and from the piercing yet opaque expression of his eyes, I could tell he would have grown up to be a soldier or a scientist, a man of great privacy and precision, and that he would have loved one woman secretly for his entire life. But nevertheless he was a child, so I tried to give him the look of recklessness and delicacy common to all eight-year-old boys everywhere.

This proved difficult, even with such a small blade.

On my way to bed, I heard a soft, rustling noise coming from the dollhouse. I got up to investigate, fearing mice. We had a problem with them last winter; Carl caught them in a shoe box and released them in the park.

But it wasn't mice. It was Otto and Gretel. They were rolling around on the floor of the master bedroom. They appeared to be wrestling.

"Give me the slingshot!" said Gretel.

"It's mine!" said Otto. "Slingshots are for boys."

"You two are being awfully loud," I said.

They froze, pulled apart, looked up.

"Who are you?" asked Otto.

"I'm Irene. I made you."

"Are you God?" asked Gretel.

"No," I said. Then I considered this. "Well, not in an absolute sense. But in reference to you, yes, I suppose so."

This had only happened once before, this coming-alive. Six months ago, I awoke to find that Drexel, modeled after the teenage son of my blue-blooded client, had stolen my charcoals, scrawled MY DAD IS A GIANT COCK-SUCKER FAGET all over the walls of the dollhouse, and fled from my apartment—probably through the fire escape. I had to completely repaper the inside, of course, in addition to replacing Drexel; it cost me nearly a week of work.

I had to admire his audacity: the real Drexel—dour, inbred-looking, personalityless—would never have dared such a thing. Also, his misspelling of "faggot" seemed oddly apt, perfectly descriptive of his father's Francophile pretensions.

Still, it was unsettling, and I didn't tell Carl. This was the second reason for keeping him out of my room: who knew when someone would come alive again? And if they did, and he saw, then what would happen?

On the one hand, I suspect that Carl would be less perturbed than a normal person if he came across a four-inch talking human: unlike anyone else I know, he believes in the inherently secret nature of everything. He believes in the dream life of penguins, in the quiet longings of plants, in the muscles and heartbeats of pre-historic fish. He eats oranges slowly, out of respect.

On the other hand, who was to say? Perhaps he'd become terrified, and leave me; or perhaps they'd go dead in his presence, and I'd have to wonder if I'd imagined the whole thing. There were too many potential outcomes, running around my imagination like wild animals, impossible to corral. One thing was certain, though: if my creations spoke to him—if these two compartments of my life overlapped and interacted—it would complicate everything, in ways I could not apprehend. It was not a development I felt I could risk.

The children asked if they could play. I told them yes, if they went to sleep in an hour.

"Let's play Pretend," said Gretel to Otto. "You be the man and I'll be the lady."

"Here," I said. "You need costumes." I handed Otto the bowler hat I'd made for his father, and Gretel her mother's shawl. Gretel promptly lay down on the table and threw her arm across her face, in a pantomime of distress.

Otto tipped his hat. "Hello, missus," he said. "What seems to be the trouble?"

"Well," said Gretel, "I have terrible dreams, about black ants crawling up my nose holes."

"Well, I am a doctor, so I can help. Do you have a washcloth?"

"Let me see." She got up and looked around the work-table until she found a stray square of cloth. "Yes. So what do I do with it?"

"You soak it in Forgetting Liquid."

"And then where do I put it?"

"You don't put it anywhere. *I* put it." He lay down on the floor, and put the washcloth over his own face.

In the morning I awoke to find that Otto and Gretel had made their way off my worktable. I followed the high-pitched sound of their voices into Carl's room—which, fortunately, was vacant; he'd already gone out on his piano-tuning rounds.

Otto and Gretel had climbed up onto Carl's turntable. Gretel stood on the record, and Otto at the base of the needle. "Are you ready?" he asked. "I'm about to do it."

"I'm *ready*," said Gretel. "Just *start*."

Otto took hold of the record with his little hands and hurled it sideways, so that it began to spin. Gretel, standing on top of the spinning record, fell down to her knees and screamed with glee. "Wheeee!" she cried. "This is the most fun I've had my whole life!"

"That's enough, young lady," I said. I brought one finger down to halt the record midspin. The two of them looked up, terrified. I could see their tiny hummingbird heartbeats through their clothes.

"We were just—"

"We got lost."

"Because we fell off the table, and—"

"Well, first of all," I said, "I know you didn't fall off. You'd be dead. I know that you shinnied down the table leg."

I was bluffing, but I'd caught them: they looked down at their feet, ashamed.

"You should know," I said, "that this room is forbidden."

They continued to look down at their feet. I thought I could see Gretel's little round shoulders shaking.

"You are going to have to think about what you've done," I said.

I took them back into my room and put them in a shoe box and shut the lid, punching a few holes for air. Then I sat down at my table and attempted to carve the clawed feet of the bathtub.

The children stayed quiet for a long time, and then I heard them mewing softly, like kittens.

I had decided to make them suffer until they learned a lesson—the last thing I wanted was for them to walk into Carl's room again—and so I tried to ignore the sound of their weeping. But I felt a growing heaviness: forcing other people to suffer, even if for their own good, has got to be the loneliest feeling in the world.

I stopped working. I sat there and sympathized with God.

• • •

Finally, I went into the kitchen, found a wide soup bowl, and filled it with sugar. I brought it back and set it down on the worktable.

"Here," I told the children, plucking them out of the shoe box and dropping them into the bowl. "You can play around in this." I quickly carved them a pair of shovels and gave them some thimbles to use as buckets.

"I wonder what it is," said Otto, sifting it through his fingers. "Is it manna?"

"What?" said Gretel.

"You know, you blockhead. The white food that fell from the sky, when the Israelites were wandering?"

Gretel shoveled some grains directly into her mouth. Her eyes grew wide. "It's sugar!" she cried.

"Impossible," said Otto. "It's too big."

"Just taste it!"

He put a grain into his mouth, and the frown on his face slowly softened. "It *is* sugar," he said, incredulous.

I pinched some between two fingers and sprinkled it down on their heads, as if dusting the top of a pie. They giggled and caught it in their palms and put it into their mouths.

In spite of myself, I smiled.

Watching them scamper through the sugar, I thought about Mrs. Perlman's family. "My grandmother never recovered from Otto's death," she'd told me. "She kept thinking she saw him. Always eight years old. Even when she was in her eighties, when her *own* kids had grand-kids. She'd go up to random children on the street and slap them in the face and yell at them in German for how worried they'd made her."

Otto and Gretel had such hard lives ahead of them, I thought; perhaps all three of us did. I felt with sudden force that I wanted to keep them, and keep them happy.

"I invented a new dance!" Gretel called out. She hurled herself down into the sugar and proceeded to do something that can only be described as humping.

"That's disgusting," I said, plucking them out of the sugar, trying to stifle a smile.

"Can you show us something else?" asked Otto, brushing the grains of sugar off his trousers. "Something fantastic?"

"All right," I said. I hunted around my desk and found a dried-up orange leaf. Carl liked to bring them home from the park when they were particularly vivid, little gifts for me from the outside world. I held it up for the children to see.

"That has *got* to be from the time of the dinosaurs," said Otto.

Carl and I met in the park. I was new to the city, and I still didn't know anything to do with my free time besides painting in my room and going to the park to sit and stare at things. So I was sitting and staring one day, and I noticed him. He sat on the ground, playing his banjo and singing softly. He wore a blue button-down shirt and a long red beard.

I came back at the same time the next day, and the day after that, and the day after that. He was always there. I felt free to stare, because he never looked up from the banjo—not once. But on the fifth day, he suddenly stood up, walked over, and sat down next to me.

"I've been watching you," he said.

"What?"

"You have very nice hands."

I looked down, as if to verify his statement. No one had ever told me this before. "But how—"

"I'm good at noticing things," he said, "when I don't seem to be noticing them. What's your name?"

"Irene."

He lifted the banjo into his lap and played "Goodnight, Irene," very softly.

Sometimes I live in the country, sometimes I live in town
Sometimes I have a great notion to jump in the river and drown

Then he got up and resumed his spot, on the grass across from me, and continued to play without looking up.

I came back every day, and sat on the same bench. Each day, exactly once, Carl would take a break from his playing and come over next to me. Neither of us would say anything; he would just sit, and play a song.

Then, one day, he packed up his banjo and slung it onto his back. He came and stood in front of me and said, "Let's go somewhere, Irene."

We went to the Museum of Fabulous Entomology, Carl's favorite place in the city aside from the park. He took me through the insects one by one, explaining why each was a marvel of creation. "This is the merifluvian Java beetle," he'd say. "It changes color upon the approach of rain, and has six distinct emotions."

When I went home, I carved and painted replicas of his favorite insects. I strung them together so that they hung, heads down, like beads on a necklace. I presented the string to him the next time we met. He stared down at it and blinked. "This is the nicest thing anyone's ever done for me," he said.

I took it from his hand and tied the string around his neck. I felt as if I were performing some tribal mate-choosing ritual. I stepped back and viewed him, the string of insects gleaming around his neck in the sun. My heart beat wildly.

We were married, officially, six weeks later.

By the afternoon, I was so caught up with the children that I forgot to listen for Carl. We were playing a game I'd devised to tire them out. It was called Run, Scream, and Fall Down.

Gretel had introduced her own modification: rather than just screaming an open vowel sound, like "ahhh," you had to scream the name of an imaginary person. Gretel screamed "Hermann Klass," "Linus Hoffenpepper," and "Frau Umbrella." Otto, clearly more cosmopolitan, screamed "Lord Kensington," "Hoopa Loopa," and "Samurai."

They were screaming "Uncle Moses" and "Hitachi Electronics" (which Otto saw on my radio and mistook for a person's name) when I heard Carl's footsteps, loud and sudden, in the hallway. He was home early.

"Shhh!" I cried, scooping the children into my lap. "Be quiet!" I placed one finger over each of their mouths.

"Irene?" Carl called.

"Yes, I'm here."

"Who are you talking to?"

"Um—that was just the radio."

"The radio?"

"Yes. It's a new program that transmits the sound of street noises from all over the world."

It was unclear to me whether Carl had heard the children or just me, but I needed to assume the worst. Through a series of gestures, I conveyed to the children that they needed to stay very quiet or something terrible would happen. I gave them a piece of paper and a pencil as high as their bodies. Working together silently, they pushed the pencil across the paper and drew a series of triangles. Each triangle was more competent than the last, and at number seventeen—a perfect isosceles—they stopped. Exhausted, they lay down on the desk and slept.

To throw Carl off the trail, I was very accommodating at dinner, practically solicitous. I found this surprisingly easy: the adrenaline of the narrow escape, and the thrill of having such a robust and vibrant secret, made me feel reckless with things I'd previously confused for my dignity.

So when Carl said, "Have you considered my question," like a statement (perhaps because he expected a disappointing answer, and did not want to signal false hope by a rising inflection), I said, "Just give me some time to think about it. All I need is some time." I was basically lying, but at the softness in my voice, I sensed him relaxing.

As we washed the dishes, our elbows touched, and I felt a new sexual charge between us. I had never thought of the elbow as an erogenous zone before, but now it made perfect sense: it's so exposed, so sensitive, so easily bruised.

Usually, after dish washing, Carl and I retired to our separate rooms to practice our respective arts. But tonight, without a word, I followed Carl into his room. He looked surprised when he turned around to face me, but not displeased. He reached out and initiated sex the way that he always did, the way that I usually liked: by lightly playing his fingers over my ear, until I nodded, giving him permission to move the wandering fingertips down to my breast. But tonight, things seemed more urgent; I took hold of his hand and moved it down to step two.

Carl smiled, and before I knew it we'd skipped three and four entirely and we were on five. We did five and then we did it again. Five, five, five.

I awoke the next morning to the sound of the children's voices.

"No, they live in *caves*," Gretel was saying.

"Everyone knows," said Otto, "that in China, dragons are pets. So they live in stables, like horses."

Leaving them to their discussion, I performed my midweek cleaning ritual, happily humming along with the vacuum. But the noise terrified Otto and Gretel. They huddled in the empty drawing room, curled into each other, hands covering each other's ears.

To console them, I uncovered the only dollhouse I'd ever made for myself: a replica of our apartment. Kitchen with tiny dining/living room area, bedroom, back room (which became Carl's; I made everything—the snow-shoes, the turntable, the banjo). There was a Carl doll, of course (red beard, blue shirt, bare feet), and an Irene (pale skin, thin dark hair, round glasses). Under the Irene doll's worktable sat a dollhouse, an exact replica, and in the bedroom of that dollhouse was another dollhouse, and inside that one, another.

I let them walk around inside. Otto and Gretel fit

right in, as if the house had been designed specifically for them. But still it was uncanny to watch them: the house had never contained anything living before.

The children dragged the Irene and Carl dolls—larger than them, but light and hollow, like scarabs—into the kitchen, and sat them down at the table. Then Gretel climbed into the Irene doll's lap, and Otto into the Carl doll's. It made an odd picture: Irene and Carl stared straight ahead, their wooden faces composed and unmoving, while Otto and Gretel squirmed in their laps.

"Nothing's happening," said Otto, after a while.

"What were you expecting?" I asked.

"Just some kind of special feeling," he said.

"We always wanted to do this with our parents," said Gretel, "but they never let us."

They continued to sit there, though, shifting positions every few seconds as if that might change things. Finally Otto sighed and said, "Let's go play."

They sat down in Irene's room, in front of the dollhouse-in-the-dollhouse.

Otto picked up the Carl and Irene dolls. "I want to make love to you," he said, twitching the Carl doll's body around.

"Otto!" I cried. "Do you even know what that means?"

"Yes," he said. "It's a way of praying. You rub your bodies together and say 'Oh God, oh God.'" He demonstrated with the dolls.

"We tried it once," said Gretel, "but we didn't feel anything."

"That's because brothers and sisters can't do it," I explained. "Also, children don't like it very much. Wait until you're older."

"When will we get older?" asked Otto.

"Well." I thought about this. "I guess I don't know if you *ever* will." The thought made me suddenly, profoundly sad.

"Will you?"

"I'm already older."

"So do you make love?"

"Yes. But not like that."

"Like how, then?"

There was a real answer to this question, but I couldn't imagine giving it. "Well," I began. "For one thing, I don't say 'God.'"

Otto nodded with understanding. "Taking the name of the Lord in vain."

They went back to playing, apparently satisfied.

That night, I pulled Carl toward me before we'd even had dinner. We were in the hallway that connected our two rooms when we started touching; after a few minutes, he murmured, "Can we do it in your room this time?"

I hesitated. We were in a rosebud-gathering, haymaking mood, and I didn't want to ruin it. And, though we'd rarely had sex in my room before, it wasn't the same as sharing a bed for the whole night. It was a step I felt able to take.

Then again, there was the matter of the children, napping in the shoe box on my worktable. But they usually napped for several hours, and they'd just gone down, so we were probably all right. And the tiny element of danger actually made me feel excited. Maybe part of me *wanted* Carl to discover Otto and Gretel.

"All right," I whispered.

Carl and I did several things differently this time. We switched the order of seven and five, and we did number eight backwards.

And it was wonderful. It was so wonderful, in fact, that I completely forgot to notice how we were positioned, not just relative to each other, but relative to other objects in the room. We were midway through a particularly vigorous number nine when Carl's foot swung out sideways from the bed and knocked off the shoe box. It landed on the floor upside down, with a heavy thud.

I leapt off the bed and started to scream. "You idiot!" I cried. "You big clumsy idiot. Get out, get out, get out!"

"But—"

"Get *out!*"

Carl dashed out of the room, naked, with an air of great shame.

I slammed the door behind him and locked it. Then I opened the shoe box.

Otto and Gretel were all right. They were sleepy and confused, rubbing their eyes, reaching out for each other, murmuring questions: "Was that a dragon? Was that an ogre? Was that a giant?"

I lay awake all night, thinking about what I'd allowed to happen. In a moment of abandon, I'd compromised the children's safety—but not in the way I had feared. How could I have expected Carl to be careful with them when he didn't even know they existed? By keeping them secret, was I actually placing them in greater danger?

I'd shrieked at him with such venom, as if he *were* a monster—a dragon, an ogre, a giant. But he wasn't a monster: just a large, gentle man attempting to love his wife.

I stayed awake all night, trying to gather courage. Was it possible to do a courageous thing fearfully? Perhaps one might propel oneself into the future even in a state of tension and panic, even with one's fingers curled in a death grip around the past.

I got up early and knocked on Carl's door.

"Come in," he said, feebly.

"I have something to show you," I said, my heart pounding, my extremities cold.

I held the shoe box out to him. Silently, he took it from

me. He lifted the lid, peeked in, and then removed the whole lid and stared down at the contents.

"Well," he said. His voice sounded puzzled. "They're beautiful."

Only then did I peer into the shoe box myself. And I screamed, a terrible scream, how I imagine Otto's mother must have screamed when she watched him slip beneath the moving train on that terrible morning—because there were Otto and Gretel, just as I'd left them, but completely inert and unalive. They stared blankly up at the ceiling with their painted eyes, the expressions hardened in their empty balsa-wood faces.

"What's wrong?" said Carl.

I took back the box. "I'm sorry," I said. "I'm so sorry." I had compromised too much, or perhaps too little. "I think I need to move out."

I moved my things into a rented room on the other side of town. A week went by. Like a delicate idea that loses its viability when spoken aloud too soon, the children failed to come alive again. Their pretty wooden bodies lay on their tiny beds, still and horizontal as corpses.

Despite my grief, I finished Mrs. Perlman's dollhouse. I wrapped the Otto and Gretel dolls, along with their parents and older brother, carefully in brown paper and twine. I had finished ahead of schedule. But I couldn't bring myself to deliver them to Mrs. Perlman, not yet.

One morning, I went to the park and found the spot

where Carl played. I sat on a large rock, from which I could see him but he could not see me. I sat and listened.

He was playing one of the songs of our early courtship:

And he made a fiddle bow of her long yellow hair
Oh, the wind and rain

It was amazing how small and far away he looked, even from this short distance. I took my hand out of my pocket and lifted it up, bracketing Carl's body with my thumb and pointer finger. I sat like this for a minute, holding him between my fingers. I held him and I held him and I held him.

Back in my rented room, I unpacked my own dollhouse, the replica of the apartment I'd shared with Carl. I set up the Irene and Carl dolls in the dining room chairs where Otto and Gretel had sat on their laps. They stared at each other across the table. I stared at them. Then I reached for my instruments.

I carved without thinking, as always happened when I did my best work. I'd begun working with no specific intention, but the little human took shape beneath my fingers anyway, insistently and specifically, as though I were simply obeying the wood's will toward a particular form. I watched *it* become *she,* a little girl, perhaps five or six years old. Her features were distinctly her own, yet resembled both mine and Carl's. She had Carl's blue eyes and my brown hair, Carl's full cheeks and my hard, inquisitive stare. There was a slight, almost imperceptible twist of impish merriment at the corner of her mouth that seemed to come from neither of us, that was entirely hers.

When she was finished, I held her in the palm of my hand and gazed at her. She was, without question, the best and most lifelike doll I'd ever created—better even than Drexel, better than Otto and Gretel. Still, she was not alive. At least, not yet.

The next morning I packed the new doll into a small nut-shaped box padded with cotton: a soft little elfin cradle. I walked to the park, hands in the pockets of my long skirt, fingers curled around my small round secret.

Carl was in the same place as always. I sensed him first, and then I saw him: growing bigger and bigger, more and more detailed, as I approached. His blue shirt, his red hair, his dear sad face.

I watched him look up, notice me, set his banjo down on the ground. I watched him stand and stiffen at my approach, wearing a look of melancholy expectation.

When we finally stood face-to-face, I grew shy. "I've come to give you something," I said.

"Something for me?"

"Yes."

"What?"

"A child." I removed the small cradle from my pocket

and placed it in his outstretched hand. Slowly, carefully, his large fingers eased it open.

We both watched, breathless, as the little girl stirred in her sleep. Then she stretched, yawned, opened her eyes.

She sat up. "*Finally*," she said, looking from one of us to the other. "I've been waiting for*ever*."

"For what?" murmured Carl.

"To be born," she said matter-of-factly. Then she leapt, like a little goat, from the cradle onto Carl's forearm. She gripped the cuff of his sleeve and hung from it, as from monkey bars, kicking her legs to make herself swing back and forth. "Whee!" she giggled. "This is fun!"

Instinctively I put my hand beneath her, so as to catch her if she fell. Carl just stared at her in wonder—then back at me, then back again at the child. This was what he'd wanted: something that was not just adjacent to me but *of* me, of us.

The little girl released her grip on Carl's cuff and dropped, like a small stone, into my hand. She looked up at us. "Shall we go home?" she asked.

Carl looked at me with questioning eyes. I nodded. "Yes," I said. "We can all go home."

Carl smiled. "Perhaps first," he said, "we should have a song." He sat down on the grass and picked up his banjo.

I sat down across from him, the little girl in my palm. She lay down on her belly, her chin propped in her hands, tiny elbows digging gently into my flesh.

She waited; I waited. The world felt very quiet, very still—an *alive* kind of quiet, the humming quiet of trees and swarming insects and sleeping penguins, of breath preceding speech. Then Carl touched the strings and began to play.

Alternate

Before Cat and I even knew each other, we were a team, knocking on strangers' doors to bring Barack Obama's tidings of hope. Everyone in Brooklyn was already voting for him anyway, so they just cheered us on and thanked us for our service. It felt like we were showing up at people's doors just to be congratulated. There was a precoital vibe, a tingling anticipation of victory. On Election Night, we stayed out way past midnight dancing in the streets of Park Slope, and when we fell into each other's arms on Cat's futon at four in the morning, it felt like the consummation of something huge: not just between us, but between us and America. It pains me to think of it now: the year 2008, the vastness of its innocence.

Neither of us had dated women before, so everything was new: this body so similar yet so other; this thrill of recognition as we passed gay couples on the street, like we were part of a secret club; and then the actual secret club. Lesbian bars, queer potlucks, dyke knitting circles. Knitting circles!

But eventually we learned a sadder kind of lesson: no matter how creative their sexual practices or identity politics, all couples fail in the same way. Barack Obama had promised us the future. Instead we got what we'd always had: the present. It was just as provisional and unsatisfying as ever, as clogged as ever with obligation and regret. Despite our best efforts to become different people, we had remained ourselves.

Cat and I moved in together, to an attic apartment in Gowanus—which, we were told, was now a Hot Neighborhood despite the fact that its single landmark was a sludgy, polluted canal best known as a site for depositing toxic waste and dead bodies.

"It's getting a Whole Foods soon," chirped the real estate agent. I nodded; Cat frowned. I loved Whole Foods: wandering the spacious well-lit aisles, marveling at how anything at all—even bread, even a can of beans—could become a luxury item, a thing of beauty and promise. I always emerged from the store with something ridiculous: a ten-dollar jar of pink Himalayan salt, a tureen of maple butter, a single persimmon. Cat, on the other hand, abhorred vanity and waste and anything corporate. She bought beans by the sack at the Park Slope food co-op, kept them in mason jars; every Sunday she cooked a huge vat of chili and ate it all week long. She didn't believe New York *had* to be expensive—not if you constantly trimmed your desires, kept them humble and well groomed and midwestern.

But the Whole Foods did not yet exist, it was just an idea—so we avoided fighting about it. It was a fight we probably should have had. Instead, we took the apartment.

Over the next year, this unfought fight grew swollen within us, like an egg full of baby spiders, eventually exploding into thousands of little scurrying fights, so many that we couldn't possibly keep track of them all. Before, the differences between us had been abstract, immaterial, intriguing; now they were embodied in the pile of unwashed laundry at the foot of the bed, the grout on the tub, the passive-aggressive sticky notes that greeted me on the mirror every morning. We never managed to settle on a decorating scheme for the bedroom. One of its walls was dominated by a large window—which had been a major selling point, though it was constantly covered in soot from the elevated F train that audibly shook the building every ten minutes or so. I wanted to paint the other walls in swirly Van Gogh pastels and stick glow-in-the-dark stars to the ceiling, while Cat wanted to leave them crisp white, like museum walls, and hang a professionally framed Rothko print. At an impasse, we did nothing; our "HOPE" poster hung over the kitchen table, Obama's face smiling in its measured yet beatific way upon our bowls of breakfast cereal, but the bedroom walls remained blank: sites of possibility that quickly became sites of curdled potential, like a blank page stared at too long.

We ceased speaking of the bedroom; we spoke of other failures. Cat was paying all of our utility bills, and my savings were running out. I grew panicked, she grew resentful, and we both privately wondered if we'd made a fundamental mistake, a mistake about the nature of hope.

Finally, one day, after we'd been living together for more than a year, I came home to find Cat sitting on our bed, staring at the blank white wall.

"What are you doing?" I asked.

"Looking at this wall," she said.

"I mean what are you doing internally."

"Trying to decide on a strategy."

"For?"

"What to do."

"About the wall? I thought we'd decided to leave it that way."

"We didn't *decide* anything. We just stopped trying."

I sensed that we were no longer talking about the wall.

"I just want to wake up one morning," she said, finally, "and look at something that's not nothing."

I didn't respond. I never would have survived as a caveman or even a cavewoman. I have no fight-or-flight-instinct, only a freeze-and-blend-into-the-background instinct. In this case, though, there was nothing to blend into. There was just us.

I stood there and silently watched as she got up, a look of resolve on her small freckled face, and began throwing clothes into a bag. I watched as she zipped the bag up, threw it over her shoulder, and gave me a long, questioning look. I continued watching, saying nothing, as she walked out the door and slammed it behind her. I watched the room attempt to settle itself, the objects stunned and mute in the wake of her sudden absence.

I could stand there for a long time, probably. My legs wouldn't even start to ache for another hour or two. Humans could go days without water, weeks without food. I could just refuse the present until it slid backwards into the past for lack of momentum, and everything was bright again.

I'd been standing there for over an hour when my phone rang. I lunged for it unthinkingly, assuming it was Cat, only to see a puzzling 301 number displayed across the screen. I took the call.

"Is this Andrea Green?" asked a chipper male voice. It sounded nonspecifically familiar, like it might once have announced a special offer for valued customers like me, or asked me to return my tray table to the upright position.

"Yes, it's Andrea."

"Hi, this is Jeremy! I'm calling from Barack Obama's office?"

"What?"

"Hi, this is Jeremy! I'm calling from Barack Obama's office?"

"Wait, Jeremy Bird? The guy I get all the emails from?"

"No. Everyone thinks that at first! My name is Jeremy Spoon. Like the utensil? Anyway, Andrea, I'm calling with some good news! You're an alternate!"

"For what?"

"The Dinner With Barack contest!"

This rang a bell, faintly: *Andrea, I am writing to invite you to dinner. Donate $15 or more today and you will be entered in the running for an evening with me!* I had responded, mostly because of the pathos of it—Barack Obama, so desperate he'd ask *me* out. Without thinking, I'd clicked on the PayPal button and donated twenty bucks, then forgotten about it.

"I'm an alternate?" I asked Jeremy Spoon. "What does that mean?"

"It means that we drew four names, and yours was the fifth. We always draw an extra, just in case! Family illnesses, freak accidents, lightning. Not to be a downer! But things happen! So hold the date on your calendar. If you don't get called, you'll get a compensation prize: a phone call from the president! Oh, and a gift certificate to Applebee's."

"Cool. I like Applebee's."

"One more thing. We post interviews with the winners on our website. And in case you end up coming, we need the same footage for you that we'll have for everyone else. So we want to come film you at your home next week—ask you about your life and your relationship to the campaign. It should be fun!"

"Yes, that does sound like fun," I said, though actually it sounded like an anxiety-inducing nightmare.

We set up a date for the interview. Which meant: in one week, a camera would come to our apartment, with America attached to the other end of it. America would stare our apartment in the face, would behold and appraise us, and our apartment would stare back.

I hung up the phone, terrified. But as I paced around the room, thinking about the phone call—its symbolic import, its strange and fortuitous timing—it came to seem like an omen, a near-magical second chance. Not only *could* I win Cat back: I *had* to.

Our relationship wasn't perfect, but it was better than any other I'd had. In the years before we met, the closest I'd come to romance was a series of drunken hand jobs I gave to one of my co-workers at Mustache Mark's, an overpriced vintage store in Williamsburg. Actually, it was Mustache Mark himself. He had a two-year-old son with a lady who brewed kombucha in her living room; despite or because of the kid, they could never decide whether to be together or not. He'd tell me about it while we closed up the store, passing a flask back and forth, and somehow his mouth would always end up on mine, his penis in my hand. He seemed to feel it wasn't a betrayal of the kombucha lady if *my* pants never came off. At least they were nice pants; I got a good employee discount. Then I met Cat and, for the first time in years, I thought: what if I didn't just take what fell into my hands? What if I actually reached for more?

Cat convinced me to quit my job there, to finish *Losers on the Roof*—the short film I'd been working on since college—and apply to film school. At first it went great. I had wind in my sails; I had Cat's hot breath on my neck each morning. But lately I kept looking at the film through an NYU admissions officer's eyes, deciding it was adolescent and bloated, and deleting half of it, only to put the missing parts back the next time. I was no longer folding and reshelving clothes, but again my life consisted just of taking things out and putting them back in.

It seemed suddenly clear to me, standing there in our bare-walled bedroom as Jeremy Spoon's words echoed through my ears, that Cat had been correct about my lapse into stagnant passivity. I'd relied on her to generate enough momentum for the both of us. But now I'd been given a second chance!

This meant one thing and one thing only: I had a one-week deadline to get the apartment ready, to win Cat back. It wouldn't be enough, at this point, to just hang her Rothko print: that would signal mere capitulation. I had to proactively demonstrate my understanding of her—her secret desires, her vulnerabilities, her hidden reserves of dreaminess—better than she understood herself. I had one week to get something amazing onto that blank wall.

I swallowed my pride and went to Ikea. I bought a track-lighting fixture and a large floor plant that, I was promised, would bloom in a matter of days. None of the pictures, though, seemed worthy of the task I needed them to perform. They all seemed sterile and self-effacing in a particularly Scandinavian way. I needed something more assertive: something American, or at least French.

I spent the rest of the day on Craigslist, looking for seductive home decorations. None were seductive in the way I needed. There were leopard-print mirrors, water-color paintings of clowns, life-sized cardboard cutouts of Miley Cyrus. And plenty of attractive, unobjectionable things too, but I could not abide the thought of choosing something merely unobjectionable—and *used*, nicked and stained with other people's failures.

And then, just like that, I found it.

Questions that ran through my mind as I approached "Tom's" apartment: 1) Was "Tom" even his real name? 2) What if he was the latest incarnation of the Craigslist

Killer? (The farther I walked from the G-train stop, the more I passed alleys and vacant lots that seemed specifically designed for the disposal of bodies.) 3) Did he even *have* a giant photograph of the Dalai Lama?

Cat was obsessed with His Holiness. She'd twice paid upward of forty dollars just to be in a room with him, and both times she came back gushing about his "presence," how he "radiated happiness" and "transcended physical space." This, of course, made me jealous. She'd recently accused me of "depressiveness," in a tone that said my dark moods, and my failure to apply to film school, were not only choices but also acts of aggression against her. I'd always seen emotions like the weather—regionally influenced yet cosmically mysterious—but Cat believed that emotions were a case of mind over mind. She was the kind of person who went running for five miles every day, even in the literal rain. She went alone to the talks; I stayed home, resentfully Googling the Dalai Lama. This gift, then, was a paradigm shift: *for you, I renounce my worldview. I renounce my right to be right.*

"Tom" lived in a converted warehouse on the edge of Bushwick; I had to check the address several times to make sure I had it right, because this didn't look like a place where a human would live. It was an empty-looking industrial building made of dun-colored bricks; a vacant lot bordered the building, separated from the street by a chain-link fence topped with barbed wire. I texted him: *Here, I think?*

He emerged a couple of minutes later: scruffy beard, knit cap pulled over shaggy hair, faded flannel shirt. He smelled like Old Spice and pot. "Yo," he said.

Who still said "Yo"? I followed him through the lot, stepping over broken glass bottles, discarded car parts, and bits of fiberglass sculpture, and he pushed open another unmarked door.

"Watch your step," he said as we entered. I looked down, expecting a high curb or wobbly stair, but it turned out he was referring to a person. Directly in front of the door, a girl was sprawled out on the floor, sleeping. She lay on her back, her arms flung out at her sides, her green dress twisted up around her middle so that her cotton hot-pink panties were exposed. Tom stepped over her, casually.

"Is she OK?" I asked.

"Oh, her?" said Tom, turning back and looking at the girl. "To be honest, I'm not sure who she is. I think she's my roommate's."

"How long has she been here?"

He shrugged. "Like a day or something."

"Are you sure she's not dead?"

"Oh yeah. She got up a little while ago and went to the bathroom and lay back down here. I think this is her way of waiting for him or something." He shrugged. "Everyone's got their thing."

"Okay," I said, gingerly stepping over the girl's body. "If you say so." I looked back; she rolled over onto her side, without waking up.

"Come on," said Tom. "It's in here."

We stepped into a large industrial space, converted into rooms for communal living by plywood partitions, decorated with everything from indie-band posters to a flaking papier-mâché sculpture of two breasts sticking out from the wall to a huge watercolor portrait of Tom Selleck.

And then I saw him, leaning against one of the dividers: the Dalai Lama, or actually just his five-foot-tall face, staring down at me.

I looked up, into his gentle twinkling pixilated eyes—and burst into tears.

Not in any moderate, tentative sort of way, either; I went from zero to sobbing like the world was ending. What I'd seen was a compassion so sharp that it hurt, that it threatened to pry me open like an oyster.

I struggled for breath through my sobs, as I pictured Cat's face, just a few inches from mine, smiling at me with the radiant love of our first few months. *You're so beautiful,* she'd said. No one had ever told me this before, at least not in a way that seemed sincere; now, I couldn't remember the last time she'd said it. But in the Dalai Lama's twinkling eyes I saw that it was true, as true as it ever had been. Somehow it was *this* that seemed sad.

Slowly I came back to myself, back into the room. Tom didn't seem taken aback by my outburst. He didn't move—just pulled out a joint from his back pocket, lit it, and took a drag. Finally, when my convulsions subsided and I started to catch my breath, he extended it toward me.

I took it, inhaled gratefully. The drug's effect was instant and powerful. I'd never felt so soothed in my life.

"I've never felt so soothed in my life," I said.

"Do you still want the picture?" he asked.

"Yes," I said. I passed the joint back to him. "Sorry about that."

"It happens," he said. "Probably your tear ducts were cramped."

"That's a thing?"

"Yeah. If you don't use them for a while, they get stiff. Like any other muscle. So then they get harder to control."

"Oh. That makes sense." It occurred to me that I hadn't actually cried since Cat had left.

"I try to make myself cry every once in a while so my tear ducts stay in shape," said Tom.

"You can make yourself cry?"

"Yeah. Watch." He closed his eyes for a second, squeezing them really hard, and then opened them. They were full of water. One tear ran down his left cheek, and then another down the right.

"Wow."

"People get really moved when they see this picture, though. Imagine if you saw the real dude. You'd probably pass out."

"I don't know," I said. "But I might get to meet Barack Obama."

"I don't really follow that stuff," he said. "I'm a libertarian."

"Oh."

"Do you want to wash your face?" he said. "You have like black streaks all down your cheeks. It looks kind of bleak."

"Sure, I guess so."

I went into Tom's "bathroom"—a toilet and sink separated from the rest of the space by a few sheets of plywood—and splashed some water on my face. When I came out, he was sitting cross-legged on the floor with two open beers in front of him.

"I once met Sting," he said, as I sat down next to him on the floor. "He's actually really short."

"How'd you meet him?"

"My sister's co-worker is his cousin. Or something. He came to her wedding."

"Really?"

"Yeah. There was karaoke, but he didn't want to sing. Everyone was kind of disappointed, but you have to give the guy a break. He does it like every day for his job."

"I guess you can't force some things."

He shrugged.

"How'd you get the picture, anyway?"

"Oh, that one?" he said, gesturing toward the Dalai Lama, as if he'd just noticed it.

"Yeah, the one I'm buying."

"I stole it," he said. I waited for him to say more, but he didn't. Finally, though, he reached for his beer.

I grabbed mine and took a long swig. It was delicious. Its effect was almost as powerful as the joint's: I felt every pore of my body relaxing and loosening. I closed my eyes for a moment. When I opened them, Tom was staring at me. No one had stared at me like this in a long time. His stare was not only sexual, it was sexual in a way that was indisputably male: that easy, unaffected possessiveness. *I want that.* It was surprising, after two complicated years with Cat, to see that look again. It was even more surprising to realize that *I* wanted *him,* too.

Before I could second-guess myself, I leaned over and kissed him. He responded hungrily, pulling my head toward him with one hand and wrapping the other around my waist. He lowered me down to the floor. Before I knew it, there was cool cement beneath me and a warm man on top. After we'd made out for a while—Tom's hands ranging around inside my clothes but not removing any of them—he whispered, "Can we go to bed?"

I thought about this for a moment. "Yes," I said, "but there are three conditions. One, you have to wear a condom. Two, I have to be on top. And three, you have to cry."

He frowned. "I think my tear ducts might be connected in some way to the ducts in my penis."

"Think of it as a triathlon for your tear-duct muscles."

At first he had a hard time getting started. He squinched his face up really tight and finally some tears started to come out. But it was like he couldn't control it. Within seconds, he was not only crying, but crying incredibly hard, just like I had minutes earlier in front of his Dalai Lama picture. I found this extremely erotic, to be straddling this sobbing man, someone who was more emotional than I was, rather than the other way around.

In ten minutes it was over. I didn't waste any time: I pulled my pants back on and held out the sixty dollars Tom had asked for in his ad.

"I feel weird taking this," he said. "I feel like a prostitute."

"I'm paying you for the picture I'm taking," I said. "If I didn't give you the money, then *I* would be the prostitute."

Ten minutes later, I was in the back of a cab, His Holiness stretched out diagonally—his head in the back seat with me, his body dividing me from the driver. I looked again into his twinkling eyes. I felt like he was smiling directly at me, across time and space, but I didn't feel like crying anymore.

Because what I realized now—what I'd cried about before, without knowing it—was this: not only was Cat not coming back, but I didn't need her to. My trip to Ikea, my Craigslisting—these were not about making a home for the two of us. They were about making a home for *me*. This was what I'd been truly afraid of, and what I was now willing to accept: I was preparing to be alone.

But when I got home, Cat was there, sitting at the kitchen table.

She was wearing a green-and-black-checked plaid shirt that I'd never seen before. Maybe she'd borrowed it, maybe she'd bought it. The latter was a surprisingly painful thought: for so long I'd intimately known every piece of cloth she put on her body. Already I knew her less, already her life had taken a small turn away from me.

"Hi," I said.

"The bedroom looks nice." She folded her arms, like she begrudged the improvement.

"Thanks. I tried."

"What's that?" She nodded toward the giant package in my arms.

"I got you a present?" I'm not sure why I said this like a question. I turned the picture toward her, so that she could see His Holiness in full effect.

She stared for a long moment, during which something happened to her: she didn't cry like I had, but the tension seemed to drain from her body. Her mouth fell open a little bit. Slowly, she unfolded her arms and raised her hands to her face.

"Oh my God," she said. "You got that for me?"

"Yeah."

"Holy shit, Andie. That's incredible."

She stood up, came over, and embraced me. She nestled her face into my shoulder. She's a few inches shorter than me; I had never dated anyone shorter before, and so no one had used this as a nestling spot before her. And now that this sweet spot was once again occupied by her face, was once again made sweet, I realized that she was prepared to forgive me for my sulking and inaction, that a small window had opened, that we might still reconcile.

And despite my resolution in the car, I knew now that I wanted her again. I wanted her warm body's companionship, her tender prodding encouragements, her gruff little snort of a laugh. I wanted to watch her screw up her small freckled face in amusement when I did something clumsy. I wanted her more than I'd ever wanted anything.

And why not? Isn't it possible to want two things at once? Couldn't I have myself and still have her?

I kissed her on the face and ears. I smelled her scalp. I wrapped my arms around her neat, narrow back. "I missed you," I whispered.

"I missed you too," she said. "It was really hard to stay away."

Then she started sniffing me. "What do you smell like?" she asked suspiciously. "Have you been with someone?" She stepped back and looked at me, folded her arms. "Have you been with a *man*?"

Now it was my turn to take a step back. I wanted to see her, see her whole body, because it struck me that this would probably be the last time I saw it in this apartment.

"I did it for you?" I said. This was true on some sort of

technical level, but I realized how unconvincing it would sound.

It turned out, after all, that some decisions were irrevocable. That I had already made my choice. My body, or the Dalai Lama, had made it for me.

Jeremy Spoon turned out to be a tiny, energetic gay man with a shock of white-blond hair; a hummingbird of a person. He bounced around my apartment, proclaiming many things special. "This quilt is so *special*. This view of the F train is so *special!*" It felt like a kind of blessing. Some priests scatter holy water or sage around a room; Jeremy Spoon scattered specialness. He was especially taken with the Dalai Lama picture. "I *love* him," he kept saying, clutching his chest. "This picture is just so *special.*"

But a few days later, he called back to regretfully inform me of the limits of my specialness. The dinner was tomorrow, and the original four people remained in perfect health; I'd forever remain an alternate. "I'm sure this is disappointing," he said.

"It's all right," I said. "I'm glad nobody died or got hit by lightning."

"That's the spirit!" he chirped.

A week later, at a prearranged time, I got a call from a "Private Number." "Is this Andrea Green?" asked a nasal female voice.

"Yes, it is."

I heard the muffled click of a switched line, and then a deep, familiar voice said, "Andrea. This is President Obama."

"Holy shit," I said. "It *is* you. Oh my God. I'm so sorry. I shouldn't have said 'holy shit.'"

He laughed. "That's all right. So, Andrea, I'm sorry we couldn't share dinner in Washington. But I want to thank you personally for your service. Without the commitment of people like you, we certainly couldn't have won."

When he said that word, "commitment," something twisted up inside of me, a knot of panicked remorse. Commitment, of course, was exactly where I'd failed. Just the night before, Cat and I had shared a final breakup dinner at Applebee's. We'd both ordered Fiesta dishes—Fiesta Chicken Salad for me, Fiesta Lime Shrimp for her—and then wept into our Fiestas and discussed the terms of the lease. I came home to an empty apartment, a short film I was too depressed to touch, a floor plant that was already dying because I'd forgotten to water it. The Dalai Lama's gaze twinkled down at me. His smile now seemed blinding and oppressive; I could hardly bear to look at him. I wanted to turn him around to face the wall.

"Andrea?" said the president. "Are you there?"

"Yes," I said. "Sorry. I just—" I took in a sharp breath, then said, "Can I ask you something? Didn't you think everything would—*change* more than it did? Or change faster?"

"Well—" He paused. I could hear him breathing on the other end of the line. I couldn't tell whether he was discerning how to distill the calculus of change into comprehensible language, or simply figuring out how to placate me, to get me off the phone. Maybe he thought I was crazy. Or maybe he took my question seriously; maybe he understood that he was the only person on earth who could.

I made myself utterly silent, waiting. The president's pause began to pulse, to take on a life of its own. The pause grew longer and longer. The pause grew until it took up the whole room.

LITTLE SISTER

I.

This story starts when my parents drop me off at my uncle Jim's house, on the way to the hospital where my little sister is about to be born. I am six years old.

Uncle Jim is married to a woman named Rhonda, whose hobby is crochet. No, not "hobby," exactly: her crocheting is a compulsion, perhaps some kind of illness. Rhonda crochets cozies not only for the extra toilet paper rolls, as I've seen in some of my friends' bathrooms, but also for the phone and the phone book and the dog and my uncle's guns and both of their toothbrushes. This cozying does not make the objects look cozier; it makes them look ashamed.

I sit all day on the sofa, the crochet pattern imprinting itself onto my sweaty legs, watching an *I Dream of Jeannie* marathon and waiting for my parents to show up and take me home. I expect this to happen quickly—within, say, an hour. No one has explained to me how long babies take to come; I have the vague idea that they just spring out, like a Pop-Tart from the toaster. Also no one has explained to me that it's way too early, that the baby is not supposed to come for two more months.

When my parents have not shown up or called by late afternoon, I begin to suspect that they are not coming back at all. When eight o'clock—my bedtime—arrives, I know with certainty that they have taken the new baby home to replace me and that I will remain with Jim and Rhonda forever. I see myself sitting here on the lumpy loveseat, becoming another permanent fixture of the house. Rhonda will crochet a cozy to encase me from head to toe, so that you can barely make out the lumpy shape of my body; I'll breathe through a woolly woven web, and will only be able to see the world in pieces, through the constellation of small apertures between the yarn.

That night in the cramped guest bedroom, fearful and unable to sleep, I create the Little Sister. I have invented characters in my mind before, fairies and pirates and things like that. This is different. I do not intend to create anything. I only try to picture the shape of this sister

I have desired and already lost, this soft human curve of abandonment, and the pressure of my need turns her real, and suddenly there she is, lying beside me on the crochet-blanket-covered bed, looking up at me with blue eyes and kicking her fat little legs. She looks like a normal baby in every way except the color of her skin—a warm, translucent gold. She smells sweet and powdery. I take her onto my lap and look down at her. She has real softness, real weight. She is a beautiful baby but I know that this is not how babies are supposed to come into the world, and her presence gives me a dark feeling. I carry her over to my My Little Pony backpack and zip her up inside. She just barely fits. Then I return to the bed and instantly fall asleep.

I awake early the next morning, to my father pulling me up off the bed by my armpits. It has been a thin, sour, uncomfortable sleep; I am so dizzy with relief to see him that I throw my arms around his neck and weep. He grunts to me and speaks a few gruff words to Jim and Rhonda. Then he carries me out to the car, throws the backpack in the back seat, and drives me home.

But my mother is not at home, and neither is the baby, because there is no baby. There was a baby, for a minute, but then it just went out. That's the phrase my father uses: "It just went out." At first I think he means that the baby got up and walked away. It takes me a minute to realize that he means the baby is dead.

I have not lost my parents, not in the way I thought I would. But I understand that things are different now. When I unzip my backpack in my bedroom that night, the Little Sister is still alive. She blinks up at me like nothing has happened, like we are guilty of nothing. In the middle of the night I sneak out of bed, take my dad's shovel from the garage, and bury her beneath the oak tree in the backyard. She does not complain or cry, but still I look away from her as I work, not wanting to watch the dirt fall onto her blue wide-open eyes.

II.

Two years later, my parents sit me down and explain that from now on they will be living in different places. This announcement puzzles me because my dad already does not live with us. He has been on a "business trip to Arizona" since my eighth birthday. This is the first time I have seen him since then. Even before he left, I had not exactly thought of him as living with us, because I no longer exactly thought of him as living. He would fall asleep in strange places, like the backyard or the kitchen floor; during his brief moments of wakefulness he would talk too loudly and hug me too hard, like a distant relative, or the Santa Claus at the mall.

"We still love you," says my mother. "I mean, *I* still do."

"Some people," says my father, "are just not cut out

to be fathers. I might have made a good uncle. This has been a whole different ball game." He leans forward, puts his elbows on his knees. "That is how I want you to think of me," he says.

"As a ball game?" I ask.

"No," he says. "As an uncle."

"I'm getting us a new apartment in town," says my mother. "It's next door to the Denny's. We'll be closer to school. And Dad will have his own apartment too."

"Why can't we stay in this house?" I ask.

"Don't beat yourself up about this," says my father. "It's not your fault."

It's an answer, but not to the question I've asked.

The night before we move, I sneak out to the backyard once again. Grass has grown over the Little Sister's shallow grave, but the spot is still visible. I don't exactly want to see her again, but the idea of leaving her there beneath the earth fills me with loneliness and panic.

I take the shovel and dig her up. She is still alive, still glowing faintly. She stirs, blinks the dirt off her eyelids, and looks at me. Her eyes glisten wetly, as if she has just been crying or is just about to, but she doesn't make a sound. I notice that she is bigger now, toddler-sized, with a round belly and plump wrists and a thick head of white-blond hair. Apparently her burial has not stopped her from growing. Apparently she is like a plant: pushed down into the earth, fattened like a root, nourished by darkness.

III.

Our new apartment does not have a yard, so I put the Little Sister under my bed, making a nest for her out of old T-shirts. She grows faster than a normal baby, faster than I do. By the time we have lived in the apartment for three months, she has corn-silk hair down to her shoulders and a mouth full of teeth. In two years she looks like a five-year-old, and in four years—when I turn twelve—she has almost caught up with me: a pretty blond girl with golden translucent skin and long limbs. She has a modest girdle of baby fat still lingering round her middle, but her limbs are lean and taut and sturdy. At night I crawl under the bed with a flashlight and pull up the Little Sister's dress and compare our two sets of breast-buds, the progress of the sparse, shadowy hair between our legs.

My mother has never discovered the Little Sister, because she never cleans under the bed. She is busy: with her job at the school cafeteria and her boyfriend, Buddy Salvage. Buddy is also known as Mr. Salvage or Coach Salvage, because he is the gym teacher. He is famous at school because he tattooed his ex-wife's name onto his shoulder and then later burned off TAMMY but not the rest of the tattoo, so that inside a heart it says I LOVE _____ and the blank is just scar tissue. He comes over for dinner three times a week and tells me unfollowable stories about wrestling and plays the "pull my finger" joke, then disappears into the bedroom with my mother for exactly thirty minutes before leaving. At school he pretends not to know me.

At night, after Buddy leaves, my mother sits at the kitchen table and makes life-affirmation collages. She cuts pictures out of magazines and glues them to sheets of construction paper. The pictures are of the mountains and the beach and other places we have never been.

"They say you have to envision the life you want," she explains.

"Who's 'they'?" I ask.

"Oprah." She takes a drag of her cigarette and replaces it in the ashtray, then cuts out a small picture of ballet slippers and tentatively places it in the center of the empty page. She frowns, then removes it. "My feet are too big anyway," she says. Then she stands up, gathers the magazines, and stacks them with the recycling by the door. She looks down at the pile, gives it a soft little kick with her foot. "The problem," she says, "is that I have the wrong kind of magazine."

IV.

When I am fourteen I get a boyfriend, or at least a boy who is sort of a friend and who I regularly allow to touch me. I like the rough texture and woody scent of his hands. I like the way he presses me down beneath him in the back seat of his car, as if it matters that I not float away.

One day, while my mother is at work, I lead the boy into my room. I know what he wants to do; I do not want to do it for the same reasons he does, but I want to take some action to prove I am an adult. While the pain corkscrews up through me I turn my head to the side and imagine the Little Sister lying there beneath the bed silently, and for the first time I hate her.

After the boy leaves I crawl under the bed. The Little Sister looks at me with her knowing blue eyes. I reach out and pinch her tiny tender right breast, as hard as I can. But to my surprise she doesn't grimace with pain. Instead, for the first time in her life, she smiles.

I get up and go to the bathroom and turn on the shower as hot as it will go. I bend over and let the hot water scour me. Then I get out, towel myself off, and crawl back under the bed with the Little Sister. I do not attempt to hide my wet salty eyes or the way my hands shake. I hold her hands in mine so that all four of our hands shake, together. She stares at me. She smiles.

That night at dinner, my mother and Buddy have one of their fights. The fight is about his tattoo. My mother believes that her own name belongs in blue ink on Buddy's arm, etched into the scar tissue where his ex-wife's name had been. She believes that she has earned this privilege by cooking him dinner three times a week for years, despite his failure to propose marriage or cohabitation.

Buddy claims that the tattoo remains an accurate depiction of his heart. He is still scarred and no amount of Hamburger Helper casseroles will change that. My mother argues that she never uses Hamburger Helper and Buddy accuses her of changing the subject. He announces that he is an honest man and that this is his best quality. He states that our mother knows this about him and has chosen him despite or perhaps because of this quality. He points out that most people, especially women, do not like to hear the truth, and he refuses to apologize for telling it. Then he gets up and leaves.

My mother walks out after him and does not come back for four days. When she returns, she is married to Buddy Salvage. His arm still reads I LOVE _____ but he has agreed to rent our mother an ornately beaded wedding dress and have their photo taken at the Glamour Shots place in the mall. The dress is large, even larger than Buddy Salvage, so large it almost swallows my mother. It looks less like a garment than a vessel. It has a skirt full and wide enough to hold several stowaways, a bodice that squeezes my mother's bosom up and out like the prow of a ship, and a veil that billows out like a ship's sail, ready to catch the wind or whatever else comes along.

V.

My boyfriend tells me that he has seen Buddy Salvage's wiener in the locker room and that it is extremely wide, like a Coke can. This knowledge is hard to suppress when I hear Buddy and my mother having sex in the bedroom next door.

At these times I crawl under the bed and torture the Little Sister. I pinch the soft skin of her inner arms and twist her breasts. I like to watch her close her eyes, silently enduring the pain, and then open them again and smile at me, like nothing has happened. Or possibly like everything has happened, like I have already done everything I have ever imagined or not imagined, so many times that none of it could possibly matter. Sometimes when I pinch her I whisper, "I'm going to kill you someday," and when I say this, she smiles biggest of all. "I'm going to drop you in the dump," I whisper, "and run off by myself. I won't tell anyone where I'm going." She smiles, as if daring me to do what I threaten, as if suggesting that this is what she has wanted all along.

But the more I threaten to kill her, the more I need her; the more I torture her, the closer we are bound together. At the end of the night I always cry and apologize; I stroke her hair and tell her I love her. She smiles again—but differently now, more gently.

One day, while we are having sex beneath the football bleachers, my boyfriend asks me to marry him. "I want to knock you up," he says, "and I want to do it properly."

I say yes, but then when I get home I am greeted by the blown-up picture of my mother and Buddy Salvage at the Glamour Shots place, framed and hanging above the mantel. I stand in the middle of the room and stare at it for several minutes. Then, without exactly deciding to, I drag the Little Sister out from under the bed, belt her into my car, and start driving.

I drive and drive, the Little Sister in the passenger seat. She has continued to grow, and now she appears close to my age; it is hard to tell, because the world has not marked her one bit. She has long blond hair and translucent gold skin and full buoyant breasts and a tiny curved waist. She looks like me, except better: how I might have looked if I'd never encountered cigarettes, or Tostitos, or birth control, or insomnia. I realize that I have chosen her: over everyone else, perhaps even over myself. I will never be able to bring myself to harm her again.

I drive and drive all night and when I run out of gas somewhere in Kansas I stop. I live in a motel until I run out of money and then I get a small apartment above a Laundromat and a job at Target.

VI.

I make the Little Sister a bed in my closet and then, when I move in with the floor manager who becomes my boyfriend and later my husband, beneath a false floorboard. The rest of my life will happen—my twins will pound across the floors with their fat sticky feet, and my husband will leave and come back and leave and come back again, and Buddy Salvage will call one day to tell me my mother has died of a heart attack, and I will drive home drunk from my mother's funeral, swerving in and out of cars on the black highway, my strange survival gone unnoticed—and no one will ever find her. She will remain my own forever. My only sister, my first and last child, my sweet secret under the floor. She will become the most stunningly beautiful old woman. She will have long snow-white hair and skin that reminds you of a Japanese lantern: lightly crinkled rice paper, lit from inside by a soft golden glow. Every day I will brush her hair, tend to her fingernails and clothes, rub rosewater into her skin.

Before I die I will do something—write a note, leave the floorboard slightly ajar—and my children will find her, delicate in death as a white moth on the windowsill, perfectly groomed and pristine. They will stroke her long soft hair and hold her cool clean hands with their warm ones and say, This was our mother's secret: how beautiful, how strange. They'll lift her from the floorboards and cradle her white head in their laps and say, Look at what she protected. Look at what she lost.

Doris and Katie

Katie O'Toole was no stranger to Oak County Hospital. She'd given birth there, four times; brought small children for broken fingers and wrists; paid post-chemo visits to her best friend, Doris; watched her husband's life flatten into a thin bright line.

And yet, on her way to accompany Doris for some routine follow-up tests, new superstitions dogged her. Everything seemed like an omen. A black bird overhead, a bag blown into the street, a sudden sour taste in the mouth. Who had thought of the phrase "routine tests," anyway? What part of this was supposed to be routine?

Doris emerged wearing what Katie thought of as her "uniform": tailored pants, black caftan, chunky silver necklace. Her sleek dark hair was shaped into a close, flattering cut. Doris had what people called "style"; her motto was "No vanity, no dignity."

"This will be the first time," said Doris, sliding into the passenger seat, "that anyone will see me unclothed. Since Fareed went." She always began conversations this way: midsentence, with no salutation.

"Oh, Doris!" said Katie.

When Doris's husband, Fareed, had passed away, nearly a year ago, she'd been in remission for six months. Underneath the "falsie," she'd told Katie, the scar looked red and shiny, like a nail polish she'd be embarrassed to ask for. Marauding Magenta, Siren Red, Raspberry Shock. At least, Katie told her, she no longer had to wear that head scarf—though it was a lovely scarf, black silk, just what a 1940s movie star might wear, given the circumstances.

As Katie backed out of the driveway, Doris extracted a compact from her purse and flipped it open. "When they find pink smudges on your teeth," she said, grimacing into the mirror, "that's when they come and take you away in the night. *That's* when it's all over."

"Ha," said Katie, keeping her eyes on the road as she pulled onto the highway. This morning she'd avoided mirrors, braiding her long silver hair in the dark. "I'm thinking of getting one of those Swedish mattresses," she said. "You know, the kind that molds to fit your body type?"

"My friend Cecile had one of those," said Doris, smoothing her hair with a careful hand. The motion reminded Katie of grooming a horse. "She said it was more sensitive than the person she shared it with."

Katie frowned, and changed lanes. "What a thing to say about her husband!"

Doris shrugged. "Who said it was her husband?" She snapped her compact shut and put it back in her purse. "Speaking of which, what did you tell Mitch Durbin?"

Katie waved a hand dismissively. "I didn't tell him anything. We're both on the library board. It's not appropriate."

"He asked you out, Katie. You have to respond."

"I suppose so." She sighed. "I just don't feel ready for all that. It's only been two years."

"And that's your choice," said Doris. "Just so you're not holding back because you're afraid."

"Who would ever be afraid of Mitch *Durbin*?"

Doris said nothing. She was staring out the window.

"If I was meant to be with someone else," Katie continued, "I would *know*. Right? Doris?"

Someone had replaced Tina at Oncology. Tina, who had sat at the reception desk and filed her nails and said, "I know, hon. I know."

The new girl looked barely driving age. Who had allowed this—her hair the color of rusted metal, sawed off unevenly at the bottom? Plus, she wore something disturbing in her ear, a kind of disk that stretched a wide hole in the lobe.

There was so little in life that one could control.

"Ahem," said Katie. The girl looked up.

"Lansing," said Doris. "I have a ten o'clock appointment."

"You can go on in," said the receptionist, flicking her electric-blue eyes from one woman to the other. "Patel's not ready, but the nurse can weigh you and stuff."

"All right," said Doris. "Hasta la vista."

Katie reached out to give her friend's hand a squeeze, but Doris had already turned away; she clicked across the waiting room and disappeared through the door without a backward glance.

Katie turned to the receptionist. "What happened to Tina?" she asked.

"Who?"

"The old receptionist."

"Oh. The one with the ponytail? Kinda chunky?"

"I suppose so."

The girl frowned. "I think she died, maybe."

"What?"

She shrugged. "They said *someone* died."

Katie found a seat on one of the waiting room's gray metal chairs and picked up a *People* from the coffee table. But it was depressing, all drug-addicted actors and grotesque human-interest stories: pretty blond survivors of sadistic kidnappings, incestuous siblings on reality shows.

She looked up. The receptionist was staring at her.

"So," said the girl. "Are you guys, like, partners?"

"We're old friends."

"Oh," said the girl, nodding. "Cool."

Katie went back to her magazine. A paragraph into an exploration of Gwyneth Paltrow's smoothie-making habits, she belatedly understood the girl's question. She felt her face grow pink.

"Old friends," she'd answered: wasn't that what lesbians used to call each other in public?

Now, it seemed, people could call each other whatever they wanted to. Her daughter Colleen had a friend who was not only gay, but in a "polyamorous triad." It had taken ten minutes of explanation for Katie to understand this arrangement, in theory—and she still had so many practical questions. Did the three men share one giant bed, or take turns? Was it a perfect triangle, or was one person the hypotenuse?

One of the three, Colleen had explained, was "the floater." Katie pictured a man in an inner tube, alone in the center of a vast, silent blue swimming pool, his tanned face tilted up toward the sun. Perhaps, in another life, she might have enjoyed such an arrangement: a glowing corona of solitude, a modest acre of freedom. In her youth there had been exactly one option: find a

AMY BONNAFFONS

person, marry him, create other people who then became your whole life. She'd had no solitude at all, for
decades—and then, suddenly, it was all she had. And
what was she supposed to *do* with it?

Yes, the old arrangement was cruel—but at least it
was simple. Was it worth it, today? All the different
options, the excitement and confusion? While devising
these new forms of sex, had they succeeded in making
it *kind*?

"Partners." Perhaps this was the best word for her and
Doris, after all. They didn't sleep together, of course. But
"friends" seemed like a hollow word for what they'd become: their lives peeled down like carrots, so that they
were the only ones left standing. Her children moving
away, with families of their own; Evan returning after
leaving her—twice—just in time to get Parkinson's; then
Fareed passing away too, a year after Evan, facedown in
the flowerbeds.

Then again, in some ways the two women were less
like partners—willing intimates—than like survivors of
the same catastrophe: thrust together yet always a bit
apart, each insulated by her own ghosts.

Katie sighed and looked at her watch. Eleven minutes.
She glanced at the young receptionist, but the girl was
otherwise occupied, staring down at a fingernail with intense focus.

Suddenly, Katie wanted to ask her all sorts of questions. Or maybe just one: *What is it like to be you?*

• • •

Two arms, two legs, two ovaries, two breasts. The body's symmetry forced you to think this way: my other one. My good one. My spare. Doris's paper gown tented above her left breast's absence as she listened to Dr. Patel's approaching footsteps.

"How are we doing?" he asked, shutting the door behind him, flashing his soap-opera-doctor smile. Later, for Katie's benefit, Doris would crack a joke—"That young doctor can probe me anytime he wants to"—something like that. In truth, though, she felt sexless as an insect these days.

"All right," said Doris. "I'm an old pro." She smiled.

He slid his stethoscope into the gown's rear opening and pressed its cold metal against her back. It was the most intimate touch she'd had in months. "So," he said. "You say you may have found another lump?"

"I think so."

He slid the instrument farther down her back. "Try to breathe like you would normally."

She inhaled. "Normal enough?"

He laughed. "Nothing seems normal when you're *thinking* about it," he said. "Why don't you go ahead and lie down."

She stretched out on the table, closed her eyes, and felt his fingers touch her skin. She opened them again when he found the lump. The doctor's brow grew wrinkled like a bulldog's, his eyes dark with alarm.

"When did you say you'd found this?"

"Oh, just a few days ago."

Actually, it had been weeks—over a month, if she was honest. This lump outweighed the one in the other breast—and a sequel, to boot. And yet she'd delayed in making the appointment; she hadn't told Katie.

There was a lot she didn't tell Katie. She didn't tell her friend about the nights she sat at home trapped in a dark mood: feeling herself slowly blending into the furniture, *becoming* furniture, hoping to become even less— as though, through sustained inaction, she might cease to be herself.

Also: once, decades ago, when Katie had taken Colleen upstairs to nurse, Doris went into the kitchen to refresh her drink, and Katie's husband, Evan, came in and turned her around and pushed her into the bathroom. She could have stopped him but didn't. She was still fuming at her own husband over his own recent indiscretion; she'd flirted with Evan all night.

She worried for weeks: counting down the days till her period, forcing herself to imagine the worst possible outcome. The scrape of the cold steel instrument, or Evan O'Toole's smug face staring out of her firstborn child's. These dark fantasies were deliberate, part of her punishment.

The other part was that she never got pregnant—not even later, when she wanted to. She told Fareed she was all right, that she only needed him. But it turned out even *that* was a lot to need. No one had warned her about this part: the lonely length of a life, the way new moments kept arriving like empty boxes on her doorstep. Each day, a fresh nothing.

Last month she'd discovered the lump and felt a strange, dark excitement. Every morning she checked it, felt the secret growing like a baby. She imagined she could feel it kick.

If Katie ever discovered this deception, she'd interpret it as some kind of misguided independence, or reckless courage. Katie was always telling Doris how brave she was. And wasn't it better, in the end, for them both to believe this—that Doris was brave?

Katie finished the Gwyneth Paltrow article and stood up to stretch her legs. For the first time, she noticed a beige leather couch out along the far wall. She walked across the room, and read the plaque hung above: THIS SOFA DONATED IN LOVING MEMORY OF DONNA HIRSCH.

Fascinating. Why, she wondered, had Donna Hirsch's family chosen this sofa, instead of a park bench somewhere, or a donation to a cancer foundation? Had they spent hours and hours sitting in this room, stranded on uncomfortable chairs? Had this been poor Donna's modest dying wish—a cushion for weary behinds?

Slowly, Katie sat down on the Memorial Sofa.

It was comfortable, but not *that* comfortable. She felt disappointed. And sorry for Donna Hirsch—was this all she'd be remembered by? A mildly comfortable sofa? She'd want more than that, if *she* died of cancer.

But no—Katie would surely live to a sad age, brittle-boned in a nursing home, sustained by sparse, pitying visits from her children. Doris would go first, with a handsome young doctor by her side. Doris would make even death seem glamorous. It angered her sometimes, what Doris could get away with.

Doris with her cheekbones and dark bob and throaty laugh. Many nights, entertaining, Katie slaved away in the kitchen while Doris told jokes, played poker with the men, raised one eyebrow in a manner Katie could not imitate (she'd tried). No matter what Katie put on the table—a Moroccan stew with exotic, unpronounceable spices, or a roast lamb that had taken all day to prepare—the party always seemed to be *about* Doris, somehow. Sometimes she'd hear one of Evan's friends remark to him, leaving, "Your Katie's a lovely woman." But she knew: none of them touched his wife in the dark and fantasized about *her*.

She stood up, leaving a slight indent in the Memorial Sofa.

Lately—with increasing frequency, since Evan passed—she'd experienced attacks of what she called "the byesies." She'd just be knitting in her armchair, minding her own business, or tending the roses in her front yard, and she'd feel the sudden urge to flee. Her heart would pound and she'd grow dizzy—until she got into her car and drove away, clarity returning to her body with the purr of the laboring engine.

Now the feeling rose up within her, as strong as ever, but she had nowhere to go. She began to pace, trying to give her body the illusion of covering distance. But it didn't work. Nausea seized her, and the room started to sway.

She sat down, pulled a handkerchief out of her purse, and began to mop her face. Soon the dizziness would possess her completely, and she would either run away or pass out. Which would be more humiliating?

"Hey," said the receptionist. "Are you OK?"

"Yes," said Katie. "No. I don't know." She lowered her head to her knees to try to stop the room from spinning.

"You look like crap," said the girl. "No offense. Listen, you probably need some air. I know this balcony." She came over, took Katie's hand, and pulled her to her feet.

Too stunned to resist, Katie let the girl lead her away. She followed all the way to the hallway's dead end, then watched as the girl opened a door marked NO ENTRY in faded yellow letters.

"Are you sure this is all right?"

"It's cool." The girl motioned for her to follow through.

The "balcony," it turned out, was a fire escape, looking out over the parking lot to the trees and hills beyond. "Don't tell anyone I took you here," said the girl. "I'm not even supposed to know about it, but my friend Ratface is a janitor on this floor and he comes out here all the time to smoke."

"Your friend is named Ratface?"

"His real name is Matthew."

They sat down. Katie had to admit, it felt good out here in the cool air. She breathed in and closed her eyes. "It's all right for you to leave your desk?" she asked.

"Whatever," said the girl. "I'm just here on community service." She pulled something out of the front pocket of her shirt. "You smoke?"

Katie shook her head. But even as she protested, she saw herself extending a hand, accepting the joint, bringing it up to her lips.

"That's it," said the girl. "Inhale slowly."

She hadn't done this since college. It was like taking fire into her body. She coughed.

"That's all right. In and out. Nice, huh?"

Doris removed the paper gown and climbed into her bra, slipping the falsie in place with a familiar motion. She used to leave secret notes here, for Fareed. One of their games. Of course, this was when she had two actual breasts. He'd stick his hand up her shirt and say, "Don't mind me. Just checking my messages."

Sometimes the note contained a joke they'd shared. Sometimes a piece of trivia, usually invented: *Did you know that duck spit cures snakebite?* Sometimes, in a mood, she wrote a simple instruction. Touch this. Do that. Now.

In their one bad season, the season of the redheaded insurance adjuster, *he* left the notes. Taped to the nutmeg jar. On the back of a cigarette pack. On the steering wheel of her car. The messages only ever said one thing. *Forgive me.*

On the day she finally did—the day she resolved to confess about Evan—she said, "I think someone left a message for you." He reached up into her bra, keeping his eyes locked on hers.

"Did you know," said the note, "that in outer space, astronauts can only open one eye at a time, or their hearts will explode?"

That was how they'd survived their remaining years: by looking at each other, but not too directly. Love, it turned out, had nothing to do with transparency, with a faithful reckoning of accounts. So much could be repaired, so much forgotten, in the alchemical heat of embrace.

Even as she got older—as her skin grew slack and her limbs heavy—Fareed still rolled toward her every morning, still sought her warm specific body. The absence of this animal heat was like losing something much larger—like losing her own blood.

Dr. Patel had recommended a biopsy. And so it would start. Her body—its stink and decay, its mutiny—would become the subject of discussion by a team of professionals, and eventually by everyone she knew. Katie would bring pie she was too sick to eat, intended to comfort Doris; acquaintances would send cards with hollow words, meant to comfort themselves. The only thing that would help was the tin of rolled joints in the back of her sock drawer—another thing she never told Katie, the rule follower.

Even amid her own crises, Doris sometimes felt a faint pity for her friend; she doubted Katie had ever known the pleasure of succumbing to disorder, of inhaling sweet smoke while the world went to hell. Fastening the final button on her shirt, Doris held this pity for her friend in her mind, like water cradled in two hands. In its presence she'd enjoy Katie's company much more; in a generous mood one might mistake this pity for kindness, or even love.

Katie pushed the door open and went back inside the hospital, leaving the young receptionist out on the fire escape. ("Just come get me if you need to, like, sign out or whatever.")

She stopped at the ladies' room, inspecting her image in the mirror to see if anything looked different. Were her eyes bloodshot? She thought so, but couldn't be sure. She'd never really looked at her own eyes that closely. Maybe that was how they looked all the time. She did feel a pleasant absence from herself, like her mind was a balloon hovering a few feet above her body. But was that really a result of the drug? Or just of the excursion to the fire escape—the thrill of a minor transgression, the way the landscape had opened beneath her, familiar yet strange?

The Oncology reception desk, of course, was empty; so was the waiting room. Surveying it, Katie experienced a brief, godlike feeling of ownership. She walked over and took a seat behind the desk, in the receptionist's chair.

Yes, she was definitely a little bit high. She swiveled the seat experimentally. She tried on a slouch, then an erect, queenly posture. She put her hand on the computer's mouse and watched the screen come to life.

She hadn't intended to actually look at the computer, but once she did, she couldn't look away. Up on the screen was Doris's chart. LANSING, DORIS. (Doris had kept her maiden name; at the time this had seemed so daring to Katie, so bold.) AGE: 65. REASON FOR VISIT:

Katie jumped up from the chair, grabbed her purse, and backed away. She looked around to make sure no one had seen; then she ran back to the bathroom. In front of the mirror, she splashed cold water on her face, over and over, hoping to wake herself up—hoping this whole excursion might turn out to be some kind of dream, or drug-induced illusion.

But no. The omens had told the truth, and Doris had not: this *was* more than a routine test.

She looked at her wet face in the mirror; it suddenly looked so *old* in the harsh, merciless fluorescent light. This was the truth: Doris had lied to her. Doris was probably dying.

She felt nauseous, like she'd swallowed something she shouldn't have, and possessed by an infantile urge to un-know; new fears and old grievances sprang up like sudden weeds. She went into a bathroom stall, sat down on the cold toilet seat, and tried to summon some of the courage she'd felt a few minutes before.

Doris returned to the reception room and found that both Katie and the teenage receptionist had vanished. Odd: Katie, like a nervous little dog, rarely moved from the spot you'd left her in.

She sat down and looked around the waiting room. She had never spent any time here by herself, so she'd never noticed its starkness. No windows, nothing on the walls. Well, all the better. It was insulting the way some hospitals tried to distract you: the fake flower displays, the paintings of European castles and people in boats. This wasn't a bed-and-breakfast. There would be no laundry service, no complimentary scones.

She leaned against the wall and closed her eyes. When

she opened them, Katie was leaning in the doorway, staring at her with red-rimmed eyes.

"So," said Katie. "How was he? I mean, how was it?"

In the car, they did not speak. Katie stared straight ahead at the road like a pilot on some singular mission. Usually, Katie would fill the car with chatter: cat litter prices at Stop&Shop, some new Japanese method for organizing closets, whatever other minutiae occupied her mind. Doris had often found this irritating, but now she wished it back. In the absence of speech she could hear the machine beneath them, all its mysterious churnings and hums. She wished for something cold with gin in it. She wished for home.

But when they stopped at the red light, at the intersection where you turned right for Doris's house, Katie turned on her left blinker instead.

"Where are we going?"

Katie didn't answer. Instead, she pulled the car over to the side of the road, put it in park, and turned to face her friend. "Doris," she said. "I want to tell you something."

Doris's heart began to pound, but she only said, "Oh? What's that?"

Katie sat still for a long moment, as if considering how to phrase a delicate confession. Then she turned toward Doris, a strange smile on her face. "Well," she said. "I'm—I'm a little bit *high,* I think."

"High? What do you mean, *high*?"

Katie let out a strange, manic giggle; then she explained how the young receptionist had taken her out on the fire escape and offered a hit. "I don't know," she said. "I don't know why I did it. I haven't smoked, in any form, in probably…thirty years. But I needed to *escape*. I just feel that way sometimes. For no good reason, really. Does that make any sense?"

Doris considered this for a moment. "It does."

"And, Doris," said Katie. "I know that *you* do it too."

"That I do what?"

"I never judged it," she said, "not one bit. I'm sure it helped you, when—well, that it's helped you." Katie smiled. "I know you wanted to be private about it. But I raised four teenagers. I'd know the smell of marijuana from a mile away."

Doris opened her mouth to respond, to defend herself—but instead what came out was a noise somewhere between a giggle and a snort. It suddenly seemed hilarious: Katie taking a prim hit from the receptionist, then confessing; Doris hiding her habit like a teenager. They might be sixty-five-year-old widows with arthritis, but they were also still the girls they'd been in that long-ago dorm, making prank phone calls in funny accents or discussing birth control in tones of hushed excitement. Suddenly they were both laughing, harder than they had in years.

"By the way," said Doris, wiping tears from the corners of her eyes, "you shouldn't be driving."

"You're probably right," said Katie.

They got out of the car and switched places. But when Doris reached down to put the car into drive, Katie interrupted the motion, grabbing Doris's hand and clasping it in her own.

"I don't want there to be any secrets between us anymore," said Katie. "You know?"

"I know."

"Don't you want that too?"

"Of course."

"So." Katie clasped Doris's hand tighter. Her blue eyes widened like a child's. "Do *you* want to tell *me* anything?"

In Katie's anxious, expectant expression, Doris could tell that there was something specific her friend was hoping she'd say. A dark feeling passed over her, like a cloud between her body and the sun. "Katie," she said. "It's been a long day."

"Of course," said Katie. "How selfish of me. You need to go home and get some rest."

"You're never selfish," said Doris. She put the car in drive and pulled out into the road.

That night, Doris sat in front of the TV, gin and tonic in hand, attempting to watch *Law & Order*. But she couldn't stop thinking about Katie's question.

Had Katie discovered, somehow, about the lump? No: that was impossible. Doris had told no one, and Dr. Patel would never have broken confidentiality. So what secret could she possibly have had in mind?

The longer Doris sat there, letting the troubling question marinate within her, the clearer the answer seemed. Katie must have known about that time—about her and Evan. She'd known for years, perhaps decades: keeping it to herself, afraid to embarrass them both by dragging it into the light. Today, a minuscule amount of weed had temporarily dislodged her inhibitions—or simply provided an excuse.

Doris and Evan had agreed it wouldn't happen again, and it never did. But the details of that night burrowed into her mind and lived there. For years, at regular intervals, they popped their heads up, like prairie dogs, and looked her in the eye. She knew what Katie's husband's thing looked like—sallow and tapered, like a melted-down candle. She knew his one-two-three, the sneer that seized his face when he came. It especially tormented her later, when Katie was pregnant again: those awful pastel maternity smocks, the great pity of her friend's innocence.

But perhaps Katie wasn't so innocent after all. She was stronger than she looked—weathering all those years of childhood crises and marital strife with a stoic smile and a stocked refrigerator. She'd probably live to be one hundred, surrounded by her complicated children and their gorgeous, life-gobbling offspring.

Since she discovered the lump, Doris had been playing

a game called Write Your Own Obit. Doris Lansing, 65, beloved high school English and drama teacher. Doris Lansing, 65, known for daring experimental productions of "Our Town" and "The Diary of Anne Frank" at Oak County High. Doris Lansing, 65, wife of Dr. Fareed Ahmed (Professor of Law, deceased), known for good jokes and impeccable poker face.

Doris Lansing, 65. Survived by no one.

Katie barely slept that night, racked by questions. Should she tell Doris she knew, or wait for Doris to admit it herself? Perhaps there was nothing *to* tell; perhaps the lump would turn out benign. No, no, it wouldn't: this was a time bomb beneath the skin, the beginning of the end.

The next morning, as soon as light began to filter through the curtains, she banished these thoughts and arose with a sense of purpose. She excelled in times of crisis: at least during the daytime, when there were things to do. She moved like a triage nurse, agile and efficient. First order of business: she'd go to Stop&Shop, buy some rhubarb and apples, bake something for Doris. It wouldn't help, but it was something to do.

While scanning the fruit aisle, though, she heard a low voice speak her name. She turned around, startled, and said, "Mitch!"

Mitch Durbin had been a physics teacher at the same school where she and Doris had taught. Now he and

Katie served together on the library board. "Listen, Katie," he said. "About that email I sent you—you don't have to—"

"I'm sorry for not responding."

"Oh, it's all right, I shouldn't have—"

"No, no. Not you. Look, I—yes."

"Yes what?"

"Yes, I'll have dinner with you."

He smiled. "I'm surprised," he said. "Surprised and pleased."

She was surprised too; she'd expected to hear herself rejecting him. She hadn't been thinking of Mitch at all, she realized as she pushed her cart away, but of Doris. Doris had been subtly pressuring Katie, for weeks, to go on this date. She'd be pleased to hear about it; it would give them something to talk about, something that wasn't *that*.

But driving home, as Katie imagined sitting across from Mitch at some candlelit table and pretending to feel whatever one was supposed to feel on a first date, she felt extremely tired. Did Doris think Katie would *enjoy* acting out these rituals of romance like some silly girl, just because it was what she herself, in different circumstances, might have done?

It was only as she pulled into the driveway that Doris's true motives occurred to her: she'd been pushing Katie toward another partner, a spare.

• • •

Back home, Katie went into the bathroom and stared into the mirror. Her hair was gray and brittle (she'd always refused dye, which felt dishonest and vain), her skin still translucent but now creased in some places, heavy in others. It was a face that bore the signs of abandonment, like some parched and weed-choked yard.

Are you guys, like, partners? Katie pulled the elastic out of the base of her braid, shook her gray hair long around her shoulders. She gathered her hair behind her head and pulled it tight; then she loosened her grip, so that the shortest layers fell close around her face. She watched her blue eyes grow wide. She had an idea.

The next morning around eleven, Doris's doorbell rang.

"Doris," said Katie, when her friend opened the door. "I made you a pie. Also, I want you to give me a haircut."

Katie bustled into the house, Doris following behind, and set the pie down on the kitchen counter. Then she reached into her purse and pulled out a pair of scissors. "You know how you always told me I should get rid of my braid? That it's too old-ladyish? Well, I think you're right."

Doris raised a skeptical eyebrow. "Are you sure?"

"Yes."

Doris sat Katie down in a chair in front of the hall mirror and arranged a fluffy pink bathroom towel around her shoulders. "How short do you want it?"

"Not too short," said Katie. "Maybe shoulder length? But, you know, do whatever you want to." She looked up, locking her eyes with her friend's. "I trust you."

Doris took the scissors in one hand and held Katie's braid in the other. She looked down at Katie, who now sat with her eyes closed and a slight smile on her face. What had prompted this sudden makeover? Yesterday's walk on the wild side, the hit on the hospital balcony? Or had Katie finally agreed to go out with Mitch Durbin? Doris had enjoyed teasing Katie about Mitch's overtures, but she'd never expected Katie to actually go through with it.

She reached down and snipped off the end of the braid, just above the elastic.

Katie gasped at the first snip, as at an unexpected electric touch. She opened her eyes, then closed them again. She smiled. She had always enjoyed the sensation of someone touching her hair, the tingling points that danced across her scalp and then down her spine. Evan had never done this. Sometimes, in bed, he'd yank on her braid, and she'd cry out. Had he thought she liked it?

Now, as the silver points danced from her scalp toward the edges of her body, she felt pricked open all over, like a sieve. It was a wonderful feeling. "This feels nice, Doris," she said. "Really nice."

With every snip of her scissors, Doris grew a little bit angrier.

She had not slept well the night before. All day, her mind had circled like a vulture: to think that Katie had watched her go through chemo, a mastectomy, brushes with death, withholding a piece of knowledge that might have set her at ease? It would have cost Katie nothing to tell; Evan had been dead for two years.

Now, to think of the months ahead. Throwing up, swallowing jars and jars of pills, lying in a hospital bed too weak to move. Katie paying her pitying visits, her mind somewhere else, with her children or grandchildren—or even, perhaps, with some new love.

This haircut, the arrogance and affront of it: how lucky, how innocent and lucky, to be able to *choose* the way your life would change.

Some red urge possessed her, and Doris watched her hand holding the scissors swoop upward, toward the nape of Katie's neck, and cut away an enormous chunk of hair. Now there was a gaping hole at the back of Katie's head.

Doris looked up at the mirror. First she saw herself: dark and pale-faced, with her scissors raised in the air; then Katie, sitting there like some tranquil martyr. She lowered the scissors again, tore them across the back of Katie's head in another wild shearing motion.

When Doris finally stopped, the woman in the chair bore almost no resemblance to the Katie she knew. Katie's silver hair was cut close to her head in the back, and in the front it jutted out in odd tufts. Doris felt a mo-

AMY BONNAFFONS

mentary thrill of satisfaction; then the thrill plummeted inside out. "Jesus Christ," she said. She heard the scissors drop from her hand to the floor.

Katie opened her eyes. Slowly, she raised a hand to her head. Then she got up from the chair and ran into the bathroom.

Doris remained in place, arms folded. She heard a sound like a choked sob, then a second one. She picked up the scissors from the floor, steeled herself, and followed Katie into the bathroom.

Katie stood in front of the mirror, staring at her mutilated reflection, tears streaming slowly down her face. She did not move; she appeared to be in a state of shock.

Doris came and stood next to her friend. She didn't say anything. What could she say?

Instead, she raised her hand, opened up the scissors, and snipped off a chunk of her own hair: a hard-won, much-loved tress that curled around her left ear. It had taken months to grow back after the chemo; now it fell to the floor, a dark little comma.

She reached over to the right side of her head, about to make a bigger, sloppier cut. But Katie, without taking her eyes from the mirror, reached up and halted Doris's hand, grabbing it around the wrist.

"Don't do it," said Katie. "Stop. Just stop."

Neither of them moved or spoke as they gazed at the strange tableau in the mirror: Katie gripping Doris's wrist, the scissors held up like a trophy. For a long time they stood and watched their joint reflection, breathless—as if the image might reveal which woman was stopping the other from moving, which was holding the other one up.

GODDESS NIGHT

I met Sharon at something called Goddess Night. I had come to meet girls. I wasn't a lesbian, but I hoped to become one.

Everyone knows now that heterosexuality isn't real, it's basically brainwashing. Plus I had heard women kissed with softer lips and knew what to do down there because they had the same business going on. Also, women probably did not do things like ask you to "play dead" and then jerk off onto your face, or if they did, they'd Obtain Consent first and it would be called Play. Men just did what they wanted and didn't call it anything. At that point I was twenty-three and I had slept with three people:

1. When I tried to lose my virginity, at seventeen, Thomas couldn't get it in. He kept saying I was too

dry. "Then just jam it in there," I said, "even if I scream. It's for my own good." But he flopped down on the shiny hardwood floor and said, "I can't do this anymore. I feel like I'm in fucking Vietnam." I don't know how many sexual partners he had had before me. He was thirty-four and my piano teacher.

2. When Tony, my TA from Freshman Statistics, took me out for curry at India Palace, I asked him about his first name, which I had always thought of as Italian and found unusual for a Korean man. He just shrugged, and I realized I had been unintentionally racist. Guiltily, I invited him up to my room. It wasn't exactly rape, because he said, "I want to fuck you," and I said, "Um, OK," but what happened next bore no relation to what I had thought would happen next. Afterward I said, "I've only had sex once, sort of," and he said, "There's no need to be ashamed of that," and I said, "That's not what I meant," but he was already asleep. I was sore the next day.

3. When I moved to Brooklyn and started working at FLOAT (Friends and Lovers of Animals and Trees), I met Ben at my local Fair Trade coffee shop. He was a software engineer from Vancouver. He wore a hemp-rope necklace with a seashell on it. We kissed on our second date, engaged in "heavy petting" on the fourth, and slept

together on the sixth. During sex he referred to my body parts by their proper medical names. He kept asking "Do you like that?" in a polite voice, like a waiter, but I just kept thinking of new NGO vocabulary words I was learning, like "low impact" and "value neutral." I stopped returning his calls.

The Goddess Night email said, "Do you feel connected to your creativity? Where are your dreams located in your body? Has your personal vision been silenced in this heteronormative, patriarchal world? Come and watch *Goddess Almighty* and discuss these questions with other like-minded women. Friday at 8, Mindy Kalman's apartment, Prospect Heights."

Mindy Kalman sat across from me in the cubicle foursquare at FLOAT. She had long frizzy hair and wore heavy, stunning, ambiguously ethnic earrings. Every day I watched her thick eyebrows moving over the low foamboard partition, like caterpillars doing a symmetrical dance.

My official job title at FLOAT was junior project manager, but it was never clear what projects I was meant to manage. Mostly I made spreadsheets. I put names into boxes—donors and potential donors—and Mindy called them and asked them to donate to FLOAT DAY!, our big yearly event where we invited one hundred low-income New York families to a spot by the Brooklyn Bridge and gave them each a small potted tree. Sometimes the name and location made them think a boat was involved, and when they found out it was only trees they got upset. But usually they took the trees anyway, so technically the event was successful.

Before FLOAT, I'd worked at a Mexican place called Don Pepito's. No one who worked there was actually Mexican. The line cooks always grabbed my ass when I walked by, and they made me wear a shirt that was one size too small because it "helped business" by making my boobs look bigger.

When I got the job at FLOAT, I was so grateful I was terrified. I resolved that the universe would never again mistake me for a Don Pepito's waitress. I made myself a twofold promise: 1) I would drink one bottle of Life Expanding Kombucha per day, and 2) I would become more generally daring. The former was to transform my life at a cellular level, as the bottle promised; the latter was to transform it at a plot level.

Which is why, when I received Mindy's email, I stood up, peered over the top of the partition dividing our desks, and said, "Um, Mindy?"

Generally I tended to avoid Mindy's half of the cubicle foursquare, because she sat next to Trent, who had perfectly tousled hair and sang in a postpunk band called Ronald Reagan's Eyeball and who I had accidentally/on-purpose kissed at the Sustainable New York Conference after-party. It turned out he had a beautiful girlfriend who made homemade lip gloss.

"Yeah?" said Mindy, not looking up from her computer. "What's up, Emily?"

"Um, I'm gonna come to your party. Can I bring apples?"

"What?"

"I mean, I'm pretty sure apples are vegan."

"Oh yeah, sure. Apples are good."

"What party?" asked Trent.

"Sorry," said Mindy, turning to face him. "It's a women-only space. Er—women and nonbinary people."

"Too bad," he said with a sigh. "I'm, like, super into binaries."

Mindy sighed. Trent smiled at me, like we had an inside joke. Sometimes we shared joke moments like this, and they killed me, though I didn't usually understand his jokes and suspected I wouldn't like them if I did understand. But he never knew what I was talking about when I tried to refer back to them later. It was part of his charisma: he went around creating secrets with other people and forgetting about them, so that they became secrets even from himself.

On Friday night we sat in a large semicircle in Mindy's living room, fifteen women and nonbinary people on embroidered pillows of various sizes. Because I didn't know anyone, I mostly kept my head down as the other guests settled into position, but I kept furtively staring at the woman directly across from me. She had emerald-green eyes, high cheekbones, and a tremendous cloud of black hair. It was impossible to say what color her skin was, partly because it seemed to faintly glow.

I wasn't the only one staring. In fact, it seemed like everyone else in the room was either staring at her or trying very hard not to. By the way she carried herself, you could tell she was used to being stared at, that not only was she comfortable in her own skin, but she also wore a second skin over her own, which consisted of people's stares, and she was comfortable in that too. When she moved—for example, raised her knee and rested an elbow on it—you could see her moving within this invisible cloak of stares, rearranging it around herself like a long flowing garment.

"All right," said Mindy. "Let's begin with a moment of silence for the women of Brooklyn and the world who could not be here with us tonight." We held the moment, silently, and then Mindy pressed Play.

It turned out *Goddess Almighty* was a documentary about two feminist anthropologists from the University of Vermont who go to live for a year among the P'Buxupi tribe. The P'Buxupi are a little-known people on a small island in the Pacific Ocean. They are completely matriarchal. The women control things like laws and trade agreements with other tribes, and the men just build huts and find food, like worker ants. Women have sex with men for procreation, but also with other women, and this form of sex is highly revered, because all women are goddesses and when two goddesses copulate the universe takes a deep breath. Or something like that. The subtitles were very confusing.

The film ended, and all of the women clapped. Two of them were crying. Then we went around the circle and shared our feelings. The two crying women went first. The first one said she had been touched by how the P'Buxupi all menstruated at the same time, in sync with the full moon, and she wished that the American women of today could do the same thing, we were so divided from one another now. The second woman began, "I was anorexic in high school." She attempted to keep going—I assumed she was going to connect this to the film in some way—but she couldn't, because she'd started sobbing again. Mindy leaned over and rubbed the crying woman's shoulder, her earrings swinging like pendulums, her eyebrows gesturing maternally. "We'll come back to you, Patrice," she said.

Then the rest of us went in turn. I was fifth. I didn't know what to say, so I said, "The film was very provocative." The group smiled pointedly at me and moved on. A gorgeous Asian woman with black diagonal bangs spoke next. "Frankly," she said, "I found the film extremely retrograde. It had all the vestiges of colonialism." She took particular offense at the scene in which one of the researchers is initiated into the tribe and then shows the P'Buxupi how to collect their menstrual blood in tiny rubber cups rather than using rags. "It's the whole White Savior complex," she said. Many of the white women nodded enthusiastically, including some who had, minutes earlier, claimed to love the movie.

A discussion ensued. I wasn't really listening. My right leg had fallen asleep, and my butt hurt from sitting on the lumpy pillow, but I felt like I couldn't get up because it would disrupt the Safe Space.

Finally Mindy said, "I want to open up the space, because some people haven't had the chance to speak yet." By "some people" she meant Sharon, the green-eyed woman sitting across from me.

Sharon had been sitting quietly the whole time, not saying anything, smiling in this thin, secret way. Sometimes, during the discussion, she'd caught me staring at her, and her eyes had laughed and invited mine to laugh with them, and I'd looked away.

Now everyone turned to Sharon, and Sharon said, "I'm just wondering how I can get a P'Buxupi boyfriend who'll build me a hut and let me slut it up with women. That sounds pretty fucking ideal." Everyone laughed, but in a strained way, because it was obvious that she was not taking things seriously.

Mindy smiled tightly. "All right," she said. "Refreshments!"

I took a strange orange-colored cookie from the refreshments table, but hesitated before putting it into my mouth. Was its color due to carrots or something more exotic? This was a question I did not really care about, but I pretended to, so that I would not have to face the daunting task of making conversation.

But then I sensed a presence in front of me, expectant and focused, and I looked up. It was Sharon, biting down on an apple wedge and staring at me with her laughing eyes.

"I brought those," I said.

"They're delicious," she said. She leaned over to the table, grabbed another apple wedge, and matter-of-factly pushed it into my open mouth. I bit down, and the sweet acid taste rushed in.

"Want to get a cigarette outside?" she asked.

I nodded, although I didn't smoke. I had asthma. As a child I wore an inhaler on a lanyard around my neck.

"So," said Sharon, pulling a cigarette out of her purse. "Let me guess. You're a straight girl questioning her sexuality."

I felt my face grow hot. "Is it that obvious?"

She smiled. "No," she said, "but I was hoping. I think you're cute."

My heart jumped up and kicked me in the ribs.

She nodded and lit her cigarette. "Yeah," she said, exhaling a perfect plume of smoke. "You remind me a lot of an Emily I used to date. Pretty but simple. Unpretentious. Like a—like a sexy pioneer woman."

I laughed. "I did play a lot of Oregon Trail as a kid."

"And I bet you never died of typhoid."

"Oh, all the time."

She patted her purse. "I'm sorry, I'm rude. Do you want a cigarette?"

"I'm OK. I don't really smoke."

"Good girl."

"So, um, what do you do and stuff?"

"I'm an herbalist. I own a small store. I sell teas, elixirs, things like that. Also some sex toys." She reached into her purse. "Here's my card. You should stop by sometime."

The card was printed on thick lavender paper that smelled vaguely of sandalwood. Above a Brooklyn address it said

EMILY
   WHAT'S YOUR DESIRE?

I looked up. "Your store is named Emily?"

"Yeah." She laughed. "Surprised?"

I said, "Do you want to come home with me?"

This is my curse. I can never do anything in a moderate, human way. It's like ridiculously extreme actions are the only way to catapult myself into doing anything at all.

I shut my eyes and braced myself for rejection.

But Sharon just laughed and said, "What are we waiting for?"

As I fumbled with my keys at the door, Sharon reached down and grabbed my ass. I felt sparks shoot through my body, which may have been sexual excitement or just nervousness.

I led her down the narrow hallway, past my roommate Helen's door (thankfully, closed), past the kitchen where we made our spaghetti and stir-fry, and into my bedroom.

As soon as we got inside, Sharon pushed me up against the wall and put her mouth on mine. It was right what they said. Her lips were really soft. She ducked her head down into my neck and kissed me there. "You're sexy," she murmured.

We went over to the bed and sat down. Sharon started to unbutton my shirt, following the openings with her mouth, kissing me on the collarbone and chest. She pulled off my shirt, then removed my bra and took my left nipple into her mouth and began to flick it back and forth with her tongue. This is when I started to laugh.

She looked up, grinning. "What?" she said.

"I don't know. I don't know."

"Does it tickle?"

"It's not that. I guess I'm just nervous."

"You've been carrying yourself so bravely," she said, and laughed. I laughed too. "Well, the thing is," I said.

And then I told her everything. I told her all about my piano teacher Thomas, and Tony and Ben, and even my Christian day camp counselor Samantha, who I think I might have been proto-sexually attracted to, because she did not wear a bra and I got uncomfortable whenever she walked by with her jiggly chest. "It all adds up to one big question mark," I said.

"You're just a cute, curvy little question mark," she said, tracing the outline of my small pale breast with her finger. "Don't worry about it, OK? Just follow your desires, and you'll live into the answers."

My breast was still exposed, its rose-colored nipple pointing at the ceiling. I didn't even feel self-conscious, lying there naked while her shirt was still on. In her gaze I felt the power of all the stares she'd absorbed, internalized and now turned back onto me. It was like an extremely flattering soft-focus light. In the light of that gaze I felt deeply interesting, glowing the way a pregnant woman glows, dense with the mystery of myself.

We talked until we fell asleep, spooning (I was Nevada, she was California). In the morning I made eggs. "I like them runny and disgusting," said Sharon, "basically on the verge of salmonella."

As we ate, we sat across the table reading the *New York Times* (me Arts & Leisure, she the magazine), like a married couple with a routine. When Helen came in, in the flannel shirt and overalls she wore to work at the organic farm in Red Hook, Sharon and I looked up, as if this were our house and Helen were an intruder.

"Um, hi," said Helen.

"This is Sharon," I said. "My—friend."

"Nice to meet you," said Helen. But Helen was terrible at hiding things with her face.

Sharon winked. "I'm not that frightening, am I?"

Helen just shrugged. "Nice to meet you," she said again, in a monotone. Helen, with her overalls and her Helga braids and her knitting. I had always ascribed myself to her level of general dullness, but perhaps I was actually more interesting.

Helen went to the sink to fill up her Nalgene bottle, and I said, "I heard those might give you cancer," and she said, "What might give you cancer?" and I said, "Nalgene bottles," and she said, "Oh." Then she left, and Sharon and I laughed as if we'd just played a joke on Helen, and I felt a little bit bad, but just a little bit.

"I have to go," said Sharon, when our laughter subsided. "But come by my store, OK? I'll make something special for you. A gift."

"What kind of gift?" I asked, but she didn't answer. She just planted a kiss on top of my head, like a mom.

"You're a good Emily," she said. And then she left.

Sharon's store was located on an easily missable side street in Gowanus, on a block with an abandoned factory, an auto-parts store, and a seedy-looking bar. The large warehouselike building was totally nondescript, indistinguishable from the other warehouselike buildings that surrounded it. Next to buzzer number 1 was a label that said EMILY. I pressed the button.

"Who is it?" came a voice through the intercom.

"Um, my name is Emily?" I said. "I'm here for Sharon?"

"Oh, OK," said the voice. "She's expecting you." The buzzer buzzed and I went inside.

I found myself in a narrow hallway smelling vaguely of urine, with a staircase covered in several layers of flaking red paint. The sign on the door to my left, made of the same lavender paper as Sharon's business card, said WHAT'S YOUR DESIRE?

I pushed the door open and found myself in a small, close room that felt more like a storage closet than a store. Brown glass bottles lined the shelves. In the middle of the room, below a single naked light bulb, was a freestanding desk, and at that desk sat a woman who was definitely not Sharon. She was fat and pretty and blond, with shocking neon-blue eyes and the most enormous breasts I'd ever seen.

"Hi," she said, smiling. "So I'm Emily."

"So am I."

"I know."

"Are you Sharon's ex-girlfriend?"

"Sharon has a lot of ex-girlfriends." She smiled, kindly. "Here. She made something for you." She reached below the desk, retrieved a small brown glass bottle, and held it out to me. It bore no markings, except for a white label with #17 written in dark calligraphy ink.

"What is it?" I asked, accepting it and frowning. "Am I supposed to drink it?"

She shook her head. "No. You just sniff it, three times a day."

"Like aromatherapy?"

"You could say that."

"What does it do?"

"It's for definition."

"Of what?"

"Your life."

"I didn't know aromatherapy could do that."

She smiled. "Oh! I forgot. I was supposed to give you something else too." She reached below the desk again, and this time produced a crumpled brown paper bag, the kind my mom used to pack my lunches in.

She handed the bag over. "It's a dildo," she said.

I pulled it out of the bag. I had never seen a dildo up close before. As an object, this one was a strange combination of girlish denial and brutal realism: it looked like

AMY BONNAFFONS

a real penis, with veins and everything, but it was made of purple sparkly plastic.

"Do you want a harness?" asked the other Emily. "To strap it on?"

"No, I'm OK," I said. I stuffed it back into the paper bag. "Do you know when Sharon's coming back?"

She shrugged and smiled. "I'll tell her you stopped by."

When I got home, I stuffed the dildo deep in the bottom of my underwear drawer. I opened the brown jar and took a sniff. It smelled like sweat and flowers. Nothing happened.

But as I did my weekend cleaning, I kept thinking about how the other Emily had handed me the dildo, so casually. I'd always assumed that my physical being (small body, flat chest, dull stringy hair) communicated certain qualities about me (a general timidity, a sturdy dependability, a guilty, diffused desire to improve the world). But if this other Emily could picture me strapping this purple sparkly plastic penis to my crotch and fucking another woman with it—then, well, wasn't anything possible?

"Short," I told the hairdresser.

"Like a pixie?"

"Yeah, but maybe a bit more—androgynous."

I watched my hair fall to the floor. The newly naked

tips of it tingled. Sharon, I thought, rolling her name around like a pearl in the wet gray oyster of my mind. Sharon Sharon Sharon.

"Nice haircut," said Mindy on Monday, her face red, her eyes averted. I wondered if she'd seen me leaving with Sharon.

"Yeah," said Trent. "I didn't know you had a face."

"I have several," I said. I puffed my cheeks out, crossed my eyes, and tilted my head to the side.

Trent laughed. "You're funny," he said.

I smiled and sat down at my desk. For once, I didn't feel the need to mentally photograph this moment; I could let it go, like a shiny little fish. I picked up the bottle of Life Expanding Kombucha waiting at my desk, frowned, and threw it in the trash. The fact was, it tasted disgusting.

But the novelty of the haircut soon wore off. Although I now looked like a person with a more interesting life, in reality everything was exactly the same as before. The same spreadsheets at FLOAT, the same apartment that smelled of spaghetti and cat litter, the same passive-aggressive arguing with Helen over the chore wheel. Every moment was predictable; every moment had an identically shaped lack. Every moment lacked Sharon.

Weeks went by. She didn't call. She didn't come by. Every night after work I sniffed the brown bottle and turned on Cat Power and tried to use the dildo, but it mostly felt uncomfortable. I could have maybe gotten more creative with it, but the fact was, I didn't really want a penis. I didn't want any specific body part of a man or woman. I just wanted Sharon to lie there and look at me.

Finally I couldn't take it any longer. Exactly three weeks after my first visit, I went back to Sharon's store.

I turned down the same side street as before and found the building, but something was different: this time, there was no buzzer labeled EMILY. The first buzzer said NO NAME LLC, and the rest of them were blank.

I checked the address again, against the lavender business card I still carried around in my wallet; it matched. I rang all the buzzers one by one, down the line, and then rang them again, going up. Nothing happened.

I went over to the window nearest the door—the one that, by my calculations, should have looked into the tiny room containing Sharon's store. But I didn't see a tiny room at all. Instead I saw a giant open space: cement floor, cinder-block walls, a few cardboard boxes stacked here and there. I walked over to another window and saw the same thing, from a different angle.

The store was gone. Like it had never existed.

There was no other conclusion. The world seemed to be playing a joke on me. This discovery accorded with a long-held suspicion that it—the world—had never quite taken me seriously. But this time, instead of resigning myself to this fact, I was filled with rage.

I went back over to the door and started kicking and pounding on it, full of petulant despair. I didn't expect anyone to hear me—I didn't think anyone was inside. This was a pure, purposeless act, the sort I hadn't allowed myself since I was a child. I needed to throw my body against a solid object, as hard as I possibly could; I needed to protest the existence of everything, the placement of everything, especially myself.

Just then, as my fists began to smart from pounding the metal door, it suddenly swung open. Startled, I pitched forward into the man standing in the doorway. He caught me, righted me, then took a step backwards, as if to brace himself against whatever I might do next. I lowered my fists, breathing hard, grateful that I hadn't accidentally punched him in the face.

"I'm sorry," I said.

He looked at me with suspicion. He was a few years older than me, tall and slim, with sandy-colored hair and round glasses; attractive in a bookish way, like a young professor, or the daytime alter ego of a superhero.

"I'm sorry," I said again. "I'm looking for Sharon?"

"Sharon, huh." He folded his arms. "Who is this Sharon? Every once in a while some woman comes by looking for her."

"Really?"

"Yeah."

"But this is her address."

"I don't know what to tell you."

So she really had vanished. I felt like I could just col-
lapse in a boneless puddle onto the floor. But even col-
lapsing was too much effort, too much of a decision. I
needed someone to tell me what to do.

"So," I said. "What usually happens next?"

"What do you mean?"

"When someone comes looking for Sharon and you
tell them she's not here. What usually happens?"

"Sometimes they leave. Sometimes they ask to come in."

"Do you let them?"

"Do you want to come in?"

"OK."

I followed him into the building. It was a giant open
space, with boxes piled here and there, like I'd seen through
the window. Against the far wall, some plywood partitions
had been set up, dividing the space into smaller rooms.

"Those are studios," the man said. "They lease them
really cheap to artists. Some kind of shipping company
owns the building."

"So you're an artist?"

"Yeah. I'm a sculptor."

"Like, with clay?"

"Come. I'll show you."

He led me over to one of the plywood-paneled studios. Sketches were plastered against the walls, tools scattered all over the floor. And in the middle of the studio,

standing nearly six feet tall, was a life-sized sculpture of a man, made out of purple sparkly plastic.

I couldn't believe my eyes. "You made this?" I managed to ask.

"Yeah."

"Where'd you get the material?"

"I found it."

I decided not to press further. "So what is it, um, about?"

"Well, it's hard to describe. But it's sort of about the female gaze."

"I've never heard that phrase before."

"The male gaze is more popular. As a concept."

"Oh."

"So this is, you know, subverting that."

"Oh."

"What do you think?"

"Of your sculpture?"

"Yeah."

"I don't know. I'm not an art critic or anything."

He turned and looked at me. "But you're a woman," he said.

I couldn't remember if anyone had ever called me a woman to my face before. Certainly no man ever had. Coming now from the sculptor's lips, the word felt obscenely descriptive, almost biblical: here we were, a woman and a man, like Eve and Adam, just two warm-blooded creatures with one fundamental difference. My woman-parts flared into awareness of themselves.

I couldn't bring myself to look at him. I kept staring at the sculpture. There was something about it that had been bothering me, something I couldn't put my finger on, and now I realized what it was. The purple sparkly man had no penis—just a smooth bump, like a Ken doll.

I turned to face the sculptor and looked him straight in the eye. "You know," I said, "I think I might have something you need."

The sex I had with the sculptor, right there on the floor of his studio, was not value-neutral. It wasn't mind-blowing, either; I didn't writhe around screaming or invoking the names of deities. But I did feel something loosening, subtly yet surely: *oh*, I thought. *So this is what all the fuss is about.* Now I knew, and there was no way to un-know it.

I knew other things too. I knew that I would never see this man again. I knew that if I came back looking for him or for Sharon, I'd find no sign of either.

I knew that Mindy would probably hold another Goddess Night, and that Sharon would not come. We would discuss our complicated feelings about the word "queer," the word "feminist," the word "vagina," the word "woman." But it would feel tired and rote, like a middle-aged couple trying to make dinner conversation. Goddess Night would not be the same without an actual goddess.

I would feel separate, as I had before, but this time in a different way. I would smile thinly and secretly to myself, because now I knew what only Sharon had known before: maybe all women were goddesses, but we were also mortals—always already dying, always yet to be fully born.

ACKNOWLEDGMENTS

Thank you to my parents, Barkley Murray and Ken Bonnaffons, both gifted storytellers, who supported me unconditionally and taught me to take risks. My sister, Blythe, helped me learn how to make things up and became a wonderful friend.

Thank you to my brilliant agent, Henry Dunow; I couldn't imagine a savvier advocate for my work. I'm grateful to Lee Boudreaux for her enthusiasm and for her smart, insightful editing of these stories, and to Jean Garnett for helping this book make its way into the world. Thanks to the team at Little, Brown, including Reagan Arthur, Carina Guiterman, Deborah P. Jacobs, Pamela Marshall, Julianna Lee, Pamela Brown, Carrie Neill, Elora Weil, Sabrina Callahan, and Craig Young.

I received wonderful mentorship from Jonathan Lethem, Darin Strauss, Irini Spanidou, Breyten Breytenbach, LeAnne

241

Howe, and Reginald McKnight. Thank you to Deborah Landau at New York University, and to the University of Georgia Creative Writing Program for providing me with a nurturing community of writers.

Thank you to the editors at *Kenyon Review*, *The Sun*, the *Literary Review*, *Southampton Review*, and *Anderbo*, for your edits and for sharing my work. Special thanks to Rick Rofihe. Thank you also to the MacDowell Colony, where some of this work was written.

Thank you to the readers who provided feedback on earlier versions of these stories, especially Axel Wilhite, Kseniya Melnik, Sativa January, Mariah Robbins, and all my other classmates at NYU and UGA. The inimitable Boris Fishman provided indispensable help with this collection, both creative and practical. I'm grateful for Helen Rubinstein's wise, unsparing eye and for her writerly friendship. David Busis is my first, most trusted, and most consistently waffled reader; I wouldn't be a writer without him. To Steve, who understands both glow and dark sparkle: thank you.

Friends, extended family (blood and chosen): dear ones, you know who you are. I'm astonished at how lucky I am to be loved by you. My gratitude to you, individually and collectively, would fill another whole book if I tried to record it with all the specificity and depth it deserves.